FAR FROM PARADISE
JAGGED EDGE HORIZON – VOLUME 2

I0623855

P.G. Baumstarck

FAR FROM PARADISE
JAGGED EDGE HORIZON – VOLUME 2

DOUBLE DRAGON

Acknowledgements

This book is dedicated to my lovely wife, Emma, and to my parents.

I would also like to thank those who read and critiqued early versions of this book and my other stories, in particular Adam S. Rowell, Adam Smith, Anne Mashimo, Brent Robinson, and Brent Smith.

Prelude - Iceberg

Mohr was trying to sleep in the transport but the turbulence kept waking him. He would just be drifting off when the jet would lurch and jounce as if they had hit a pothole. Nearly 150 years since man had first acquired wings, he thought, and the sky was still a bumpy road.

The transport's hold was filled with the other men of his platoon. None had said a word since lifting off, as they were all dampened by the surprise news of defeat. Colonel Kurkland had delivered the news that morning at reveille: the Home Guard War was over. Officially the settlement with the Norwegians was being branded as a 'ceasefire,' but the terms had more the ring of a 'humiliating surrender.' Mohr's men were also bearing the brunt of the shock, as they were being flown back to Oslo only an hour after roll call. They had awoken that morning thinking of themselves as soldiers still engaged in a desperate struggle, and now it was not even lunch and they were being carted off as post-war surplus.

While Mohr was depressed like everyone else, he was also partly relieved. After the war's rocky start, he had been anxiously awaiting news of their first big victory. But this had never come. The reports had stayed an endless stream of convoys being blown up, bases being harassed, and engagements being denied. And yet the brass had let

7

it drag out, first for one month, then two, and then even for a few weeks more. At last it was over.

Mohr glanced over at Janus sitting next to him. He texted—to not have to shout over the jet noise—, ">Think this is the end of the army?"

Janus looked back. ">Has to be," came his swift reply. ">What do you think this war cost? / One billion? / Two?"

">*If that* ... " Mohr shook his head.

">And now they're still just throwing in the towel."

">Yep ... / Even if the whole company's not going under because of it, / I can't imagine the army has much chance of being profitable after this. / Probably nothing left to do but split us up and sell us off."

">That must be why we're all collecting back in Oslo / the fire sale," said Janus.

">Ah, right. / Our transport sets down on an auction block / and the bidding starts before a panel of security contractors."

">And world dictators."

">Heh, yeah."

They had posited that as a joke, but, as Mohr considered it, the more likely it seemed. His grin faded.

">If it came to that, what would your choice for next gig be? / Africa? / South America? / Asia?" Mohr was trying to salvage the joke.

">Well, definitely not South America, all those jungles ... / And definitely not Africa, there they got jungles *and* deserts. / Though southeast Asia has jungles, too, I guess ... / Fuck, I don't care where, just *no jungles*—that's my only rule."

Mohr chuckled.

In the hold there arose some excited chattering from the men. Mohr and Janus looked around but saw nothing to explain it. When they checked the transport's forward cams, however, they understood: they were at last approaching the city.

For many of the men, this would be their first sight of Oslo. They were slobbering over every angle coming from the transport's external cams, and some were even looking out of the windows— to behold the original photons. Mohr thought this irreverent, but he could not blame them. There were several modern ruins, but none with the combined mystery of Oslo.

The low-rise sprawl of the city's outskirts lay ahead, painted a pallid mien by the sullen and overcast day. This sight alone would not have been exceptional had it belonged to any other city, but the mere knowledge that this was Oslo made it fantastic and eldritch. Coming closer, all the city's conspicuous absences came into focus: no cars, no lights, no movement. Trees and greenery were everywhere growing wild, terrorizing the streets. And the buildings were all dilapidated and speckled with broken windows.

Approaching the city center, the heights of the buildings climbed through low-rise, mid-rise, and incipient high-rise levels. But where the city should have had its crowning island of arcologies, in Oslo there was a strange void. The buildings were absent from so large a space as to suggest an impact crater. Inside it, every lot was piled high with debris, yet the streets had been cleared for the corporate army's vehicles. It was a strangely manicured city of rubble.

They soon neared the location of the corporate army's base in the old St. Hanshaugen Park. The last time Mohr had seen Alpha Base—as it had been called back in the early days—it had been just a cluster of buildings with a heavily defended perimeter. Over the years he had heard of it being turned into a hardened installation and renamed 'The Bunker,' but that was all. He was curious what had become of it, as this was his first time back to Oslo in four years.

At first sight of the base, Mohr was stupefied. The Bunker was a squat nanometal dome dominating the center of the park. Its featurelessness at first yielded no sense of scale, but, comparing it to the few surrounding buildings and control towers, Mohr gauged that its footprint was larger than ten square blocks. Its ground level was ringed with eight, massive, twenty-meter–wide hangar doors, all of which were open and ferrying in great tides of men, vehicles, and supplies as if into eight sacrificial mouths. The surrounding oblong expanse of the park had been thoroughly paved to create 'St. Hanshaugen Tarmac.' Everywhere were transports and heavies landing and dusting off, and in between disgorging men and cargo into the teeming maze of ground traffic. Mohr looked for any tents or temporary structures set up on the tarmac, but there were none. Everything was going inside the Bunker.

He had not thought about it that morning, about what it would mean to have the entire corporate army relocating to Oslo. But if at least ten thousand men and all their attendant supplies were going to fit in there, then that structure had to be greater than even that stupendous dome. That had to be only the iceberg peak of a staggering underground complex. Something with the rackspace, garages, messes, food stores, heads, infirmaries, gymnasiums, vid theaters, sim farms, and even the whorehouses and distilleries to sustain an entire division underground for weeks.

Turning to Janus, Mohr repeated his opening question, now rife with self-sarcasm: "Think this is the end of the army ... "

Janus huffed and shook his head at the astounding scene. "Now I wish it had been. 'Cause, otherwise, this ... " he gestured out the window. "*This* can only be the beginning of something tremendously fucked."

Chapter 1 - Second

As the *Jotunheim* neared the rendezvous, her first sensor contact came in the form of one of her forward drones sighting a drone from another ship—like two advance scouts from separate armies meeting. The drones interrogated each other and verified that they were friendly, and so Frisch knew that they had found the Human fleet.

After registering with the net, sensor data from the eleven other Human ships was streamed to the *Jotunheim*, and her own vision was added back. Tacspace came alight with the wide gathering of friendlies. Their ship took up position in the fleet's standard three-layer formation: heavyweight carriers and battlecruisers in the center; cruiser and destroyer screens rotating around those; and finally a much thicker valence of probes and defense platforms extending out in all directions.

The *Jotunheim* was the last ship to arrive, so all of the captains now convened in a simspace meeting. Frisch and the other commanders appeared with Commodore Hadamard around a circular table. National emblems hung behind each of them, with Hadamard's Confederation seal shining subtly the brightest—to signify his command.

"Good to see you all in one piece again, ladies and gentlemen," said Hadamard. "Cards on the table."

Frisch realized this meant that they were to share the cryptographic keys to the sections of the sensor grid they had just laid. After doing this, a holo appeared over the table showing a projection of the unified grid. Each probe appeared as a dot on the surface of a great sphere, with its visibility drawn around it as a breath of light. The completed net was a lambent shell woven around the Hezokeen position. None of the near- or mid-range probes showed any contacts, but the long-range ones dimly revealed hundreds of Hezokeen ships lurking at the center. Also shown were the recorded tracks of past Hezokeen patrols, which came arcing out of their fleet core like stellar prominences. A counter at the bottom of the holo showed that all 2,013 probes were online.

"Excellent," remarked Hadamard. "So, we discussed our strategy back planet-side, but, now that we're out in the field, let's recheck the tactical situation. The grid's up, so now the next move is the Hezokeen's. And they have a limited number of options.

"First, even though we've surrounded their fleet with a sensor grid, this is still *space*, so they could try to pick up and move away. But the grid's sensors are all hyperspace-capable and could move with them, so the Hezokeen would just end up with two thousand probes chasing them. They won't try that.

"That leaves the other option, which is to try to destroy the grid here in a pitched battle. If they can take out enough of the sensors to fracture the grid's

13

coverage, they can make an escape. That's what we can most likely expect.

"Now, it looks like the Hezokeen haven't spotted the grid so far, but, once they do, we can expect—" Hadamard broke off when he was interrupted by a sidechannel. He was looking off as he read something. "Set condition red and prepare for immediate scramble. Meeting adjourned."

Oh fuck, thought Frisch. He snapped back to the *Jotunheim's* tacspace context and relayed the brief orders. The bridge officers pressed around him, eager for details.

«What is it, Captain?»

«We've got no contacts on the screens ... »

«Did Hadamard say anything?»

Frisch flashed them negative responses while he checked the sensors himself. Their immediate vicinity was clear, and the grid showed no activity from the Hezokeen fleet ...

«Did anything happen while I was in the meeting?» Frisch asked. «Anything at all?»

«Well ... » said Kittelsen. «There was this weird signal that came from Earth. Computers analyzed it—just a mathematical sequence. Probably someone running a hypercomm test. It was a little high-power for that, though.»

Frisch first dismissed that. But then it struck him as a second thought: a mathematical sequence ...

Hadamard soon came on the comms, fleet-wide address:

«I'll keep this short. Just minutes ago we intercepted another rogue hypercomm transmission. This one was cast from the Earth in the direction of the Hezokeen fleet. All of our comm systems would have seen it and discarded it.

«I've talked with Fleet, and they've confirmed that this had the same characteristics as the first pirate signals some weeks ago. Only back then it was the Hezokeen fleet that spoke first, and their Earth-side agents who replied. The signal just now was cast first from the Earth, and the Hezokeen fleet hasn't responded yet. Since they're maintaining comm silence, HQ thinks there's a fair chance this might have been the 'go' code for some operation. Possibly an invasion. Our main fleet is already mobilizing for that eventuality.

«So let me be clear: we are on high alert, poised to oppose an all-out invasion by the Hezokeen. Even though the MINDEFs didn't want to lower the Space DEFCON to two—just in case this turns out to be a false alarm—the entire fleet is to act like it. All ships in flight are scrambling to emergency battle rendezvous, and everything in port will put to the skies within the hour.

«Our job is to watch the sensor picket and provide any forewarning and profile of a Hezokeen move. To do that we'll be fanning out, every ship for itself, to watch the lines. Patrol in strict stealth and investigate any possible contacts from the grid. We'll maintain comm silence, only breaking it in case of a confirmed Hezokeen sighting. —And

15

that's a *mass* sighting. I don't want anybody sending back 'Zulu-Echo-Zulu' for just a five-ship patrol»

Frisch dimly recalled 'Zulu-Echo-Zulu' as the priority code for an *en route* invasion of the Sol system. He remembered a day in officer candidate school where they covered 'common three-letter emergency codes for events that will never actually happen.' But now one of those was actually being invoked ...

«If we see nothing from the Hezokeen within twenty-four hours,» Hadamard continued, «then we rendezvous at Point Kappa-Niner. But stay sharp. If there really is an invasion on the way, Fleet will need as much warning as possible so that they can start evacuating cities Earth-side. *That's* our job here: sight the Hezokeen, save lives. The second we get a confirmed sighting, we run Plan Lima back to the system and join up with the fleet.

«If there are any questions, we'll be out of whisper range in a minute, so make it fast. Other than that, good luck, and good hunting»

Once the channel closed, Kittelsen announced to the *Jotunheim's* bridge: «NAV: Dispatch orders received: / Patrol grid branches Victor through Tango»

«CO: Proceed / speed: stealth +0.5»

With their ship on its way, Frisch could finally react to this change of stakes. But he was still stupefied—an *invasion?* They had not even seen an alien ship first-hand on this mission yet, but, if what Hadamard had just said were true, then not five

16

minutes from now the Hezokeen fleet would set off on a straight shot for the Earth—and their own puny flotilla would be the first thing to be swept aside.

In tacspace the Human ships were splitting up, and the great mass of probes and plats was breaking back down into individual accompaniments for each vessel. The *Jotunheim's* engines were still hot from the ride in, so she was quickly making her way out from the rendezvous, climbing back up to a lonely place along the grid.

Chapter 2 - Obsolete

Hanssen waited till the next morning to jet back to Leknes. When he lifted out of Bergen, the sun was hanging low but determined in the sky, the day already hours old from its perspective.

Steffens called once he was in flight. Hanssen had been wondering how everyone back in Leknes would take the news of the treaty.

"Cassie?" he answered the call.

"Haze, good—we're glad you're coming back."

Keying on her tone, Hanssen looked at her with concern.

"It's the Brigadier."

***

Following the last leg on his OHUD map, Hanssen ended up outside of the Brigadier's hospital room. He entered softly and approached Krohg's bed, where the man was propped up to receive visitors. Thin tubes ran between his face and arms and some attendant machines. These were all blank of displays—their data available only over privy hospital augspace.

Krohg turned towards him. "Hanssen ... " he said, his voice an intrenchant whisper.

"Sir." Hanssen sat in the chair next to the bed. "How are you?"

"Better, better ... It wasn't so much the aneurism as it was the ... falling down afterwards. ... 'Falling

18

down,'" he repeated with a laugh-like exhalation. "No way for a professional soldier to go."

Hanssen tried to grin but accomplished nothing. "I've ... talked to the doctors. They said they patched you up, but that you won't let them administer a simple OPN treatment to make the cure permanent." One of Krohg's sons had caught Hanssen in the waiting room and explained the obstacles the man was offering to his treatment. Hanssen had agreed to talk to him about it, if only to find out his reasons.

Krohg chuckled to the limits of his ability. "'OPN treatment,'" he echoed. "I don't even know what that means."

"Sorry, it's 'Out-patient nanome—'"

"No, no, I know what it *means* ... But what *does it* mean, really?" He gave a sarcastic puff.

Hanssen drew back. "Then is your objection some ... religious thing?"

His eyes drifted down. "Perhaps. I suppose it's a 'religious thing' whenever we act on belief. And sometimes contrary to reason."

"... So you're against the level of technology or—"

"No, no, I'm not against the technology. Far from it ... " He turned to look out the window. He struggled to muster his ever failing voice, "It just feels like this world ... Like *this world* ... isn't mine anymore." He sighed. "I mean, how could it be? With space elevators, and alien embassies, and ... " A hoverbus flew past. "And hover-*everythings*," he gestured choppily outside.

19

He looked back to Hanssen. "I just feel that, wherever humanity's going ... *its* future ... isn't mine anymore. And the longer I wait around the more alien *I'll* become."

Hanssen looked down into his hands. He could see why Krohg had not wanted to explain this to his children. Maybe he was only telling Hanssen because he was accustomed to taking what Krohg said at face value, without arguing or reinterpreting. Yet Hanssen did feel called to say something contrary, as if Krohg were contemplating suicide and he had to talk him back from the ledge.

"But of course it's your future. Everyone's ... future," Hanssen said thinly. "And don't you want to see how we get through all this? Leknes and the corporate army? With Norway still in pieces. And the depression? Don't you want to see if the world ... "

Krohg raised a hand weakly, dispersing Hanssen's words. "The human race will get through. It always does. Even if some parts of it don't. And now I only want to see the end of my life the way I always thought I would. Or as close to it as I can get."

Hanssen remained silent for a minute more. He did not know if he would pass Krohg's reasons along to the man's son, waiting outside. If at all, he could only present it as something simple and neutered. 'He thinks it's his time.'

"Thank you for coming to see me, Hanssen."

"Of course, sir. ... If there's anything I can—"

20

"You've already done it. Listened."

Hanssen stood to go. He caught the man's eyes. The glance was solaced but also held an eager, inner spark. He covered Krohg's hand where it rested on the bed, giving it a departing grip.

"Take care," said Krohg, turning back towards the window.

Out in the hall, Krohg's son looked to Hanssen. "Did you ... " he started.

But Hanssen only shook his head. And the man understood. Hanssen left.

Hanssen remembered meeting Krohg five years ago during the Singularity's recovery efforts. At the time the Brigadier had found him as another wreck among the ruins. He had offered to take him back to Leknes and employ him there, to let him heal at his own rate. Yet in all the time since they had never shared any breakthroughs, and Hanssen was afraid the man might think that he undervalued their connection. So Krohg making this confession to him at last felt like an affirmation of their unspoken closeness. He knew what Hanssen could not say, and did not blame him.

But the meeting had gone entirely differently from Krohg's perspective. He had opened up to Hanssen only because sometimes deeply personal facts could only be discussed comfortably with strangers, and that was what Hanssen was to him. Krohg had taken Hanssen back to Leknes to let him open up, but with that never happening Hanssen had stayed a distant charity case to him. To Krohg this meeting only reaffirmed their distance, and at a time when it was too late to be changed.

***

Soon afterwards Hanssen received two messages. The first was from the Brigadier to the Mayor, CC'ed to him, announcing his resignation for medical and personal reasons. The second was a reply from the Mayor, appointing Hanssen as commander of Leknes's Home Guard, and promoting him to a full Colonel accordingly. Remembering his duties, Hanssen scheduled a conference for later that day—he still had to discuss the ceasefire with the men.

But until then he walked around Leknes, and finally ended up in his usual booth in Lutefisk's, overlooking the bay. By then the sun had breached the zenith, at last tipping the day's scale over from new to old.

Chapter 3 - Chess

"Since the Hezokeen fleet appears to be on comm silence," the Chief was saying to the assembled ISSO agents, "Fleet Command is afraid that this might have been the 'go' code for an invasion. ... That's right: an *invasion*," he reiterated. "Which means our worst-case scenario has suddenly become one where there's a Hezokeen fleet sitting in orbit lobbing down plasma-nukes."

Townsend's attention had a tendency to drift during telepresentation meetings, but the Chief's last statement had focused him—as intended.

"If the Hezokeen are on the move, Fleet has told me it would take them around twelve hours to reach the inner system. Our own fleets would be outnumbered three- or four-to-one and so couldn't engage them directly. Instead our plan would be to wait and fight in the inner system where we have the Lontan defense grid backing us. Now, if that grid performs up to all of the Lontans' promises about it, then we should have nothing to worry about. But, to be on the safe side, once the Hezokeen were eight hours out, the world leaders would order a general evacuation. So, what—"

"Excuse me, sir," interrupted an agent.

"Yes, Durbey?"

"A 'general evacuation'—evacuate *what*, sir? The *planet?*"

"No, just the cities. That would thin out the population density and mitigate the casualties in case a warhead hit."

Townsend balked. He knew his job was to protect against certain alien threats, but the orbital bombardment of his home planet was not usually enumerated among them. He would work harder otherwise.

"So, what can we do in the meantime?" the Chief posed. "Well, I wish it were more, but the investigative work we do takes time, and there's no way we can ramrod everything through in twelve hours. And sooner than that an evacuation might be ordered that would send the world's entire population running for the hills. And, even if we can capture the hypercomm and its operators within that time frame, they've already sent their fleet the attack code. So their job is done and we're too late.

"Which is why we're not going to treat this like it's the end of the line. This may not be a full invasion after all. It's only been twenty minutes, but so far their fleet hasn't moved. And, if they don't invade now, that means we get another chance. So I need us all at one hundred percent starting now to make the most of that chance.

"Before you all split back off, are there any questions?"

Agent Fakenham asked, "Did the Lontans get any better localization on the source of this signal?"

"Ah, I'd completely forgotten ... " The Chief gestured to the lone mannequin present. All of the

Human agents assigned to Operation Mal Voisin were attending this simspace meeting, but the Lontans had sent only one of their own to represent the 'hive.'

The female model spoke up: "Unfortunately no, Agent Fakenham, we did not. This signal had just as advanced scrambling on it as the first. But, if we assume that both signals were broadcast from the same terrestrial location, then we can combine our intercepts for better localization. Here is the result, although it is still not of much use."

The room's holo showed the localization trace of the first signal—the great, oval-shaped stamp over Europe—plus the new one. This second trace was only half the area of the first, but it still enveloped Spain, France, Germany, the UK, and bled off into Italy and Scandinavia.

"If they keep sending signals from the same location," Fakenham asked, "I'm assuming this localization will keep improving? Eventually we'll know where they are?"

"Yes," said the mannequin.

"How many more intercepts would that take?"

"Two or three, if we're lucky. But even then it would only be narrowed down to an area the size of a city."

After a lull, the Chief said, "Now if there's nothing else ... let's get to it."

To Townsend, the meeting simspace blinked away and he found himself seated back in his

Stockholm office. He swiveled around in his chair to face Zhang. "*Fuck*," he exclaimed.

Zhang pursed his lips.

"Is there really an invasion on the way?"

"At present, no. But it has only been twenty-three minutes since the signal. That is perhaps too early to expect the Hezokeen to have moved. Especially if they have been sitting idle for all these weeks."

"How long then?"

Zhang shrugged. "They could be mobilized in a few hours."

Townsend turned back to his desk. He began flipping through information frantically, consumed with the idea that he alone had to turn back this invasion. Even with the all-powerful Lontans on the case, he still felt there was some room for Human effort. Despite the Lontans' undeniable superiority, there were always scenarios where an inferior method could yet be the better tool.

He felt this was especially true in their field of crime solving. Here the Lontans were perhaps like Hercule Poirot: they could always find their man, but it might take them days of excruciating analysis and drawing room maneuvering to do so—time they no longer had. But meanwhile the Humans were like Dirty Harry: all they needed was a gut instinct about whom to shoot in the kneecap, and—if they guessed right—a confession would fall out pat as a theorem.

Townsend flipped through the intercept reports on the pirate hypercomm signals. Skimming the details, he said,

"So this latest signal ... the contents were identified as the 'Catalan numbers'? ... And then the first two messages weeks ago contained some 'Mersenne primes' and a 'Dashouk ensemble'? What is this—two mathematicians sending each other love letters?"

"Not quite," said Zhang. "The sequences are mathematically defined, so they can carry no novel information by themselves. The Hezokeen must be using them as a simple one-to-one code with pre-arranged messages. Sending the Catalan numbers may mean 'attack' or 'prepare' or even 'withdraw.'"

"Then it's impossible to guess what these messages mean?" Townsend reasoned. "Even if this wasn't the 'go' code, we won't know what it will look like when they send it?"

"Correct."

"Still, couldn't we try ... mimicking their broadcasts? Spam them with the Fibonacci sequence or something?"

"We could, but we would only be shouting out words from a foreign dictionary. We would have no idea if it would mean anything."

"Yeah ... " Townsend slumped down. "And then what are the odds that we'd hit on the exact message that meant 'Never mind; go home' ... "

Zhang shrugged and said, "Slim."

Townsend looked at him. The mannequin sometimes had a deaf ear for rhetorical questions.

"Well, still," said Townsend, sitting back up, "couldn't we ... jam the channel their agents are transmitting on?"

"No, their transmitter is much too powerful—it has to be to get a signal out twenty light-years. We couldn't drown them out even if we had every hypertransmitter on Earth broadcasting noise at full volume."

Townsend sighed, abandoning that route. He looked back through the reports and brought up the maps showing the terrestrial source of the two signals.

"So, these ovals that show the likely points of origin ... " he began afresh. "They cover a lot of area, but, well, this latest oval is *centered* on Belgium. So can't we just assume that the hypercomm is there and work from that?"

The mannequin nearly frowned. "That's not precisely how probability works, Agent Townsend."

Townsend smirked, knowing he had only been playing 'moron's advocate' with that. He was about to speak again when Zhang preempted him:

"If I may, Agent Townsend, these issues are being addressed by people with far more knowledge and expertise than yourself. Meanwhile the Chief asked you all to focus on your specific investigations into the Hezokeen's terrestrial agents."

"Fine, you're right. So what have we got there?"

"Well ... " Zhang said uneasily, as if a bluff had been called, "in our case we've followed all of our leads. We can only wait until our surveillance yields something more."

"What?" croaked Townsend, dark and incredulous. "First you tell me to get back on the tracks, and now you tell me the train isn't going anywhere?"

"That is the state of the investigation."

"No. The state of our investigation isn't 'Hurry up and wait,' because, if it is, it only means we need to try something else to get it moving again."

"What do you suggest?"

Townsend scowled. "Well, *you're* the all-knowing God-Lontan. *You* tell *me*."

"I assure you, Agent Townsend, that we have tried all investigative routes."

"And *I* assure *you* that I'm not just going to sit here till the end of the world. And you're going help me scare something up." He stood and crossed to the wallscreen decorated with all their investigation's notes.

"Even if this signal means nothing and the Hezokeen are not invading," Zhang urged, "we still have no way to further our—"

"Stop talking. I'm going to go through all of our leads, and, for each one, you're going to tell me why the only thing we can do is stick another finger up our asses."

"Fine," Zhang nodded, and swiveled around to face him.

Townsend began flipping through the headshots and surveillance stills they had adorning the wallscreen. "What about ... Sly Tierney, the American mobster."

"Actually, the more we tie in, the less relevant Tierney's already dim correlation becomes. We have dismissed him."

Townsend had learned that 'to tie in' was the most important verb in Lontan investigative work. The idea was that, while Sherlock Holmes could solve any crime with only three crucial facts and a great leap of perspicacity, the same could be achieved by simply collecting billions of random facts until the truth became obvious—the old 'quantity versus quality.' Thus Lontan procedure was to slop all of their raw information into some stupendous computational Crockpot—the 'tying in' part—and to poll it for answers as if it were a Magic Eight Ball. Here Zhang was saying that they had dumped some more Exabytes in and, when they had asked it about Sly Tierney, it had replied, 'My sources say no.'

Townsend pulled up the next headshot: "Dmitry Kalmagorov, the Ukrainian."

"We might have had some chance there, but Kalmagorov looks to have been assassinated. He dropped off the nets thirty-seven hours ago."

"Maybe we could find him?"

"We suspect he was mulched."

Townsend grimaced. So the atoms of Kalmagorov's body were mortaring a Kiev arcology by now.

He went to the next picture: "Peder Kjaerstad, the corporate army CEO."

"He has some leads that may be of use to us, but we must wait to see if he moves on them."

"Fuck waiting; let's *make* him move on them."

"We covered this before. Such brands of influence are highly illegal," Zhang turned admonishing.

"Hell, I don't mean to rewire his brain, but we can still *talk* to the guy and get him to work with us, can't we?"

"... You wish to recruit him?" Zhang was surprised.

"Well, obviously."

"How would you accomplish this?"

Townsend nearly rolled his eyes. "Hell, I don't know. Threatening him with jail time, threatening to blow the whistle on him to Lindon, appealing to his sense of civic responsibility—come on, work with me. Why is this so hard to follow?"

Zhang shrugged. "In Lontan first contact operations, investigators operate under the directive of 'Look; don't touch.' Surveillance and information gathering are typically not allowed to interfere with the subjects they are observing."

Townsend rolled his head backwards and chuckled mordantly. "You know what you Lontans' problem is? ... I'm sure you have the technology to

31

read all our minds and solve every crime instantaneously, but you have all these first contact rules that say why you can't do that: violating people's rights, respecting noetic privacy, and dot fucking dot. So with all these rules it becomes a *game* to you: 'Enforce the law with some specific set of techs and rules and capabilities; *go*.'

"But the point isn't to play some game. It's to *bust skulls*, *make arrests*, *get results*. So yeah, we're not going to maneuver Kjaerstad to do what we want through some elegant, fifty-move–deep strategic gambit, but the point's not to think of that gambit—it's just to checkmate the motherfucker however we can.

"So come on, I want to talk to this Kjaerstad stooge because I think I can get him to work with us. But the clock's ticking and I need a way to do it that won't tip Lindon off so that he can pass a warning on to his smuggling contacts. There has to be something in the Lontan arsenal that'll let me do that without violating any laws."

Zhang paused for a second, during which he was engaged in a lightning information exchange with the Embassy. Once finished he said simply, "You are quite right, Agent Townsend. And I have just received approval from the Embassy for such a method. We could try as soon as you're ready."

"... Oh," replied Townsend, caught off guard. If he had been arguing with a full-blooded Human, he would have expected Zhang to at least enter a brooding fit before acceding. Yet the mannequin had displayed an egoless malleability to reason.

"However," Zhang added, "I believe we should contact Kjaerstad's Mafia contact, Zuzanna Mukhina, instead."

"Ah, right," said Townsend, recalling that, on the Kjaerstad–Mukhina ticket, *Kjaerstad* was the pretty face. Mukhina was the one who had procured the information they wanted, and so she would be best able to carry this forward. "Let's ring her up."

Chapter 4 - Up

Willoch was woken by the chimes as the space elevator car pulled into the cavernous docking bay at Gateway's nadir. Up through the window she saw the neon-lit terminal, which was a stark change from the black void that had held there for the entire voyage up.

She sat up and felt around for her belongings ... before remembering that she had brought none. Lev tickets were charged by the gram, after all, so she never brought bags, never wore heavy clothes, and even fasted for a day and got a haircut beforehand. Regardless of how cheap energy and transportation had in general become, the lev was still hauling things straight up into the air, and investing even a pack of peanuts with 20,000 kilometers' worth of potential energy had an irreducible cost in Megajoules.

Her floor's exit led to a gangway escalator that ferried her up to the main concourse. After clearing customs, Willoch unexpectedly saw Commander Nielsen, one of her subordinates, standing ahead in uniform. This was odd: Nielsen never waited for her to come off the lev. And there was something awkward about him, too—the way he was looking for someone concertedly ... And when he spied her there was too much obvious relief in his face.

Something had happened.

Willoch quickened her pace, almost to a jog. Nielsen met her as close as he could and the two formed up, heading for the nearest entrance to the military legation. They remained silent, as they could not share any details until they were in a secure space. Yet in the meantime Willoch heard many suggestive snippets from the ambient conversations:

"Yeah, all the dockers got called away, some surge need down in the military ports ... "

"—sorry about the delay, ma'am, but the military's been preempting the flight lanes all afternoon ... "

"—officially they're saying it's an 'exercise,' but you know what—"

Each of these tantalizing hints gnawed at Willoch. And, when they finally reached an entrance to the military section, she saw a Human guard posted outside of it. That was a procedure they only rolled out with the highest alerts—they were possibly already at DEFCON 2.

Once inside, Nielsen said hurriedly, "There was a second signal—another pirate hypercomm burst—this one from the Earth, to the Hezokeen fleet—same style as the last—"

"How long ago?"

"Five hours."

"*Damn,*" Willoch swore. She was only hearing this now because she had been stuck on the lev for the last nine hours, whose comms were too insecure to carry such sensitive information.

"The signal was the same style as before," Nielsen continued, "only the Hezokeen fleet hasn't responded to this one."

Willoch could draw the obvious conclusion, and she made sure they were steering for the situation room.

"Any word from Hadamard?" she asked. She had logged into the secure net, but it would take her nontrivial seconds to find these answers herself.

"Yes, and so far there's been no major moves from the Hezokeen. His ships are combing the sensor grid and will sound any alert."

"No '*major*' moves?" Willoch asked, picking up on his word choice.

"There has been a spike in the number of Hezokeen patrols since they spotted Hadamard's grid—about an hour after the signal. They set up some hammers in their fleet core, but, other than that, they haven't budged."

Willoch's tension was eased. But still she muttered, "The whole system staring down an invasion, and I've been stuck in that tin can for the last day ... "

"Yes, ma'am, and I looked if there were some way to get you up here faster," Nielsen began racing through a prepared spiel of excuses, "but those cars run at their max speed as is—and they don't have any escape pods or anything on board—and there was no way to send a ship down to dock with it—so then I thought—"

"Fine, fine," said Willoch, pardoning him.

36

When they entered the situation room, Nielsen peeled off to man one of the stations at the room's periphery. Willoch proceeded to the center depression and its twelve chairs arrayed in a circle around a large holodisplay. All of the seven other Eyes admirals were in attendance—three of them physically and the rest telepresenting.

"Admirals," Willoch greeted them. "Please excuse my attire; I'll change once I feel apprised of the situation."

"Quite all right," Admiral Jeremy Lightman replied.

"Nice haircut," added Suvorov.

That he could make a joke told Willoch that the mood was not as dire as she had feared.

The center holo held the definitive tactical view of the system: every installation, starship, patrol drone, and sensor buoy as far out as the Human species could see. From a glance, Willoch saw that just over three quarters of the fleet had reached alert positions around Persephone orbit. That was far enough out to be in an attack posture, but still close enough to be able to pull back to the inner planets in case of any surprises. The remainder of the fleet was still launching from Gateway and the other shipyards.

Willoch next checked that their auto-defense platforms were garrisoning the inner system. The Lontans had assured them that these platforms could protect everything inside of Mars from even the largest Hezokeen attack. But Willoch's confidence was hard to gain there. She only trusted their Lontan ships because they had Humans—such as herself— at their helm; but as to automated platforms ... There were reasons why the verb 'to Skynet' had entered the Human vernacular.

Finally she checked the Monitoring Lines—the fixed sensor nets covering everything out to three light-years from Sol. These showed no bogies on approach. And, from Hadamard's small bulb of sensors staked farther out in the void, she could see that the Hezokeen fleet was stationary. Everything looked secure. Even if the Hezokeen moved now, they would still be half a day getting to the inner system, and the entire Human fleet would be long stood up by then.

"So the fleets are almost done scrambling," Willoch observed, "but I still see a lot of civilian ships out there."

"We decided not to ground civilian spaceflight just yet," Admiral Ibuka answered. "All of those ships can put to port inside of six hours, which leaves plenty of time to order it, even after the Hezokeen have moved. And we didn't want to cause any more panic than we already had."

Willoch nodded. "Any planet-side preparations?"

Lightman answered for everyone with a sardonic shrug. "We've done what we can, but ... before this we'd barely even considered what to do in case of a planetary bombardment. Some of our countries have army and national guard units scrambling just in case, but we can only pray that they won't be needed."

"The leaders will order an urban evacuation if necessary," said Admiral Cao, "but, with our level of preparedness, it'd be a catastrophe just trying to control the Human traffic. We'd cause tens of thousands of casualties just by ordering it, so we'd better not do so unless those lives are in danger to begin with."

In her OHUD Willoch checked the alerts that had been cobbled together by the other Eyes: all strange cocktails of domestic drills and emergency directives ... Though she knew that one country that would not have issued any alerts at all was Norway. With no national government and no chain of command, they simply would not have been CC'd on any of the disaster mailing lists. Maybe Bergen would have been told, but there was more to Norway than just that city.

So Willoch drafted a message for the governors and the senior Home Guard commanders herself. Though she kept it vague—no details about the Hezokeen or an invasion. The Home Guard may need to know about the emergency, but they were also notoriously leaky. So far they had miraculously avoided setting off a worldwide panic, and Willoch would not see her country shattering the calm.

Chapter 5 - Relay

Lieutenant Linz rose to his feet, asserting himself over the din of the conference room:

"Then I want to know what was the *point* of the whole Lindon campaign if we just ended up *giving* the corporates Oslo in the end?" Other Home Guard officers echoed his question in murmurs.

Hanssen thought Linz's tone was more direct and irate than he would have allowed for speaking to the Brigadier. In fact most of the men were still treating Hanssen as if he were only their executive officer. Of course he had not thought they would adapt instantly to him as their new CO, but he also knew he could not politely wait for them to come around.

"Remember, Linz, what the Brigadier said at the start of this campaign," he answered coolly. "Our goal was not to obliterate the corporates to a man—that would've been impossible. Just as it would've been impossible to drive them from Norway completely. We could only ever have gotten concessions from them, and we just got the best concessions we possibly could have. That was the point of the campaign."

Hanssen's mention of the Brigadier—and his Krohg-like composure—made Linz realize he was speaking to his new commander. His expression faltered, and he sat back down.

Steffens, at Hanssen's side, added, "And, Linz, have you *seen* the long-range scans of Lindon's superbase in Oslo? There was no way we could have challenged the corporate army there. So they were keeping that, regardless of anything else we did or negotiated. So the Colonel's right that this treaty is the best possible outcome, because the Bunker is just about the only thing they *are* keeping."

Hanssen glanced at Steffens. He had expected her to be one of those most hostile to the treaty, yet she had been at his side—as just then—from the start of the meeting. After his promotion Hanssen had tapped Steffens to be his XO, and she doubtless knew that an XO who quibbled with the CO in front of the staff did not long retain their post.

Liljedal spoke up next from the audience: "Okay, sirs, so we weren't going to take back Oslo with *this* campaign, granted. But with this treaty aren't we giving the city to them forever? It's theirs to do with as they please now, and we're saying we won't ever challenge that."

Hanssen and Steffens looked at each other, both hoping the other would handle this difficult question.

They were saved from this predicament when Roscher's telepresence abruptly dialed in to the back of the room. His appearance drew everyone's attention, like the intrusion of a drunken relative at a wedding. He looked over the assembly, walked up to Hanssen and Steffens at the front, and slyly took a seat next to them.

"Colonel," Roscher greeted him.

Hanssen realized what he was doing. Back when Krohg had been in charge, Roscher had always known to stay away from these meetings. But, now that Hanssen was in charge, Roscher was testing the waters of upward mobility. And that loud "Colonel" had been Roscher hoping to trick Hanssen into calling him 'sir' in front of everyone.

"'General,'" Hanssen parried his advance.

Roscher gave him the slightest sideways squint in return.

At least Liljedal's awkward question about Oslo was not repeated. That covered the price of Roscher's admission—this time.

A lieutenant directed the next question to Roscher: "Since we have an official peace now, 'General,' might I ask what the ANP's plans are?"

Roscher appraised the man with a stern look. He let the audience hang in uncertainty for several seconds ...

"The ANP is staying on board," he replied with sudden casualness. "At least until we're sure that this ceasefire will hold. I should say that we'll be satisfied after about ... two or three weeks." He glanced at Hanssen again with his dead eyes.

Hanssen decoded this to mean that Roscher's Revenge had an ETA of 'two or three weeks.'

While the next question was being rattled off, Hanssen received an urgent message from Admiral

Willoch. He signaled Steffens to take the lead while he read it in his OHUD:

FROM: Willoch, Lene ADM, MINDEF
TO: Laurantzson, Ousland, Brechts, Feiring, ... , me, ...

The admirals and I are handling an emergency up here on Gateway, and it's possible that the situation could extend down to the surface. In preparation, military forces around the world are going on alert, and Norway should not be left behind. I can't provide any details, but I advise all Home Guard commanders to stand up your units and prepare your contingencies for evacuations and humanitarian disasters. I will send an all-clear after the danger has passed.

After reading it once through, Hanssen's first thought was, What the hell. He imagined this was code for an impending meteor strike. The black-water navies were scrambling to shock a surprise asteroid off a collision course with Earth, but, failing that, everyone would have to run for the hills and seek shelter while the granite rain started to fall.

He considered calling Willoch for confirmation ... but, if that was what all the other recipients of this message were doing, then Hanssen would get stuck on hold. And, even if he did get through, what would he do but ask her the same moronic questions everyone else was: 'What is this about?' 'Is this for real?' 'Are you sure, ma'am?'

Instead he took the initiative. He stood and said, "Meeting adjourned—but everyone stay online. I'm going to have a snap announcement for you. Cassie," he said to Steffens, motioning her off to the side towards the adjoining conference room.

The audience responded with some searching glances. Half of the room stood and started calmly for the exits, while the other half—those telepresenting—winked out of augspace, although they kept their links to Leknes active.

Hanssen forwarded Willoch's message to Steffens—Willoch had sent it only to him and to Krohg, obviously unapprised of Leknes's recent change in command. Hanssen waited until Steffens had finished reading it, which she indicated with a,

"What the fuck."

Hanssen shrugged as if to say, 'Now you know as much as I do.'

"Did you get confirmation?" Steffens asked.

"If Admiral Willoch sent it to all these people, then that's all the confirmation I need. I think we should hop to."

Steffens shrugged. "So ... what do you want to do? Kick-start an all-out drill and ... fire the civil defense sirens?" she suggested randomly.

Hanssen's features hardened slightly—a negative reply.

"Then ... how about just the Home Guard running an exercise? Like something out of the old disaster prep plans?"

Hanssen grumbled positively this time, but also with a lilt that said a bit more was needed.

"So ... maybe we coordinate with a few city agencies as well? Get them on board discretely so that they're ready in case this goes full bore?"

Hanssen at last grunted.

Steffens could see how being his XO would be: positing orders by trial and error until she earned his approval. Just so long as it worked.

"Yes, sir. I'm on it."

Just before she was out the door, Hanssen called, "—Oh, and congratulations on your promotion, Lieutenant Colonel."

Chapter 6 - Hammers

This last alert had played out exactly in line with Frisch's previous military experience. First, *panic*. A second pirate hypercomm signal was intercepted, a Hezokeen invasion was imminent, and the Earth's only chance was to respond with skyrocketing alert levels and disintegrating contingency plans. Everyone hurried to their assigned positions, gritted their teeth, and ...

Second, nothing happened. No intensified Hezokeen patrols. No net fleet motion. Nothing even to write home about, let alone issue a 'Zulu-Echo-Zulu' for. Anticlimax.

The only thing that had happened was, after an hour, the Hezokeen had at last noticed the new Human sensor grid around them. They had dispatched some patrols to scope out its coverage, and then they had turned on some hammers in their fleet core. These were hypernoisemakers that pumped out an antiphony of wide-band static, which denied their long-range sensors of any detailed surveillance. Before this their sensor grid had been able to count the Hezokeen ships individually, but now the enemy core was shielded as behind a fog. Still, far from embarking on an invasion, all the Hezokeen had done was erect a privacy screen.

Now, five hours since the alert, the disquieting calm still held. The *Jotunheim* was pacing through hyperspace at stealth speeds, attending to the jitter on the sensor grid like a spider to its web. Their duty remained to watch and wait.

«Sir!» flashed Kittelsen.

—Ha! Frisch crowed: something worthy of his attention.

Kittelsen pointed to some new arrivals on their section of the grid: four small Hezokeen groups. Two contained heavy ships with escorts, and the other two were formations of fast-attack destroyers. The Hezokeen patrols had hitherto consisted only of corvettes, so these four coordinated groups spelled something different.

Frisch highlighted the heavy bodies in tacspace. «What do you think those lead ships are?» he asked his crew.

«Arsenal ships?» suggested Khlebnikova.

«Hammers?» said Kittelsen.

This last guess was confirmed when the heavy ships burst with twin shockwaves of hypernoise. This was a more concentrated version of the noise that was screening the Hezokeen core. In tacspace the noise bursts appeared as expanding spheres of static, opaque to all sensors. The spheres enveloped the other Hezokeen ships—thus masking them to the Human sensors—and continued expanding towards.

The hammers' shockwaves quickly dissipated as they neared the frontline probes in the Human sensor grid. Just as the noise thinned enough to become transparent, the hidden Hezokeen

47

destroyers burst out at unexpected locations. The wall of static had masked their approach, and now they sallied out, hoping to catch the Human probes by surprise and destroy a few. It was an obvious tactic.

But the tactic being obvious also meant that it would not work. The drones in the Human grid were each controlled by a limited AI that was highly protective of its own existence. And they could infer the Hezokeen's intentions easily. So, as soon as they had seen that wall of static approach, they had backed out to a safe range. When the Hezokeen destroyers emerged from the shroud of noise, the Human probes were well away and continuing to recoil so as to deny any chance at a shot.

«The Hezokeen aren't going to bag many probes that way ... » commented Khlebnikova.

«And, even if they get a few,» added Bruun «we did drop *two thousand* of them. They should figure we have some spares on hand»

«Maybe they're just testing how the grid responds to intrusion» said Kittelsen.

«Or they might be trying to stretch it out ... Punch a hole through it»

That last was a possibility, Frisch saw. The Human probes were too smart to be destroyed by this simple tactic, but their backing away was slowly opening a hole in the grid around the Hezokeen intrusion. As the Hezokeen drove inward, their hammer ships fired again, and the Human probes backed away again, carving out a deeper salient.

But, zooming out, Frisch saw that the Hezokeen could not use this tactic to punch a hole all the way through the grid. Already more probes were pulling themselves from the near sections of the grid and forming up around the Hezokeen bulge. Once the enemy ships were deep enough inside, the probes simply reconnected behind them, pinching the Hezokeen off as if in a vacuole. Only if the Hezokeen stacked up a dozen of these groups operating in sequence might they be able to carve a continuous breach through the grid, but they were obviously not trying for that. Frisch had to wonder if they intended something else ...

Chapter 7 - Escape

Peder's eyes passed over the many sultry women circulating beneath the dim lights of the soiree. There was a powerful magic in low light that made it a prerequisite for gatherings such as this. It shielded people's defects and emboldened their vanity. It lent an anonymity that was the essential ingredient for moving boldly and fearlessly. And it cast a confidential air under which all pleasures were permissible.

Up until a few months ago, Peder had been a frequent participant in hookup parties such as these. This was where the upper class went to find their one-night stands, their mistresses, and their supermodel escorts. He had always thought of these as shallow and vulgar, and—once he had had his fill—he had finally sworn them off as beneath him. Yet now here he was again, amidst the damned.

His reasons had started back when he had learned that Lindon Securities was going bankrupt. It had taken a while for such an outlandish fact to set in, since this was not just a simple bankruptcy but an impending fiduciary doomsday. With the scale of Lindon's debts, Peder's company would most likely be liquidated and he and all his men sold as chattel slaves before the creditors would be appeased. It was the end.

Until that moment, Peder had marveled at his ability to escape the depression. Every year attendance at the posh cocktail parties shrank, and the frivolous charity balls grew less extravagant. Peder had had close friends whose wealth had all vanished within a week. And those who remained behind would never discuss the fallen, for fear that doing so would call down the jinx on themselves. But now it had at last caught up with him.

Hence why he found himself at this posh hookup party at Sloan Masterson's flat, looking for one last hurrah of pleasure. No matter how low it was, he rationalized, was it not the only thing left to him? And with false humility he thought that men could never fully reform their actions. At best they could adopt a cycle of abstinence and orgy, saving up their good behavior only to justify eventually cashing in for some bad.

Soon after arriving he was approached by Sloan Masterson. As host, the man was required to interact briefly with each guest. Though etiquette dictated that, whenever two men addressed each other at a hookup party, any conversation longer than three sentences was tantamount to courtship. Hence Sloan spoke only in passing:

"Ah, Peder; good to see you. Been months, hasn't it?"

"Sure has. Take it easy, Sloan," said Peder, waving good-bye to the already retreating man.

Soon in Sloan's wake followed Natasha Crimsky—the first woman to approach Peder that night. He was annoyed by the intrusion. If he had left before this he could have still counted the night

51

as 'no harm done,' but speaking with Natasha made his trespass official.

"My, my, if it isn't Peder Kjaerstad," she opened with a simpering, lascivious grin.

"Tasha, wonderful to see you," he replied mechanically, and the two shared kisses on the cheek.

Negotiating a hookup was a delicate task. Neither person was looking for any component of a relationship; more of a fencing partner in the domain of genitalia. Hence getting to the point was desired, and so the man had to be fast and direct. But, as this most certainly was not about fencing, he also had to be excruciatingly subtle and *in*direct. A woman might be the most promiscuous in the world, and yet to negotiate sex from her without a veneer of double entendre she would still consider an impertinence.

Despite Peder's years of practice at such negotiation, he was still only an intermediate. Granted there was plenty of alcohol and recreational narcotics available at these parties, but negotiating under their influence was often more difficult than not for him.

Yet, as he and Natasha spoke ... he was surprised by how well he was doing. He was surely not out-performing a class-A player, but he was doing well above his par. —Especially for having so little heart in it.

Was that what he had always been doing wrong, he wondered: *caring?* Reveal your desire for

52

a woman, and then she already knew you for her conquered slave. But, if one instead behaved to a woman as if she were a boring irritant, then she would be cozened into intimacy as the only way to break through the apathy and salvage her self-esteem. ... Actually that made perfect sense.

He was coming awfully close to bringing Natasha to the culminating point of their negotiations ... but ultimately he failed. He had not been able to close the deal after 30 lines, and if not by then, it was not happening. They said their good-byes, and Natasha returned to her tour of the room.

Analyzing his performance in postmortem, Peder decided it had been his own surprise at his success that had ruined his chances. Losing his shield of apathy had made Natasha warm with a realization of conquest. Then she had been done with him, off to her next triumph.

Despite that failure, Peder felt how good it was to be back. He had come here full of dread and self-loathing, but now he was having fun. ... Granted he was only pandering to his limbic system, but it was amazing how sudden and positive his psychological reaction was.

Though with immediate dismay he found his thoughts drifting back to the problem of his coming downfall. He momentarily toyed with the idea of placing a put option on Lindon's stock, to at least secure his own fortune and survival ... But he had to reject that. Even the dumbest neural nets the financial regulators had sleuthing the grid would be able to flag his activity as insider trading. And, while there was always a crackdown of regulation after a major shock, now five years into the depression it was practically a capital offense.

Another woman approached him: Secily Alaia. Natasha had drawn him out, and now the rest of the pack was taking nibbles at him.

Peder received Secily coldly and shone on her the same hassled attitude he had given Natasha. And, just as with Natasha, he was negotiating strongly. ... In fact, within only 20 lines he had succeeded. He had to say but one more word and they would be ten minutes away from a much better acquaintanceship. He was startled to have succeeded so easily, and in the past he would have been thrilled at the chance to score someone like Secily.

But he slyly pulled back. His self-confidence and jackass-hood were growing by the moment, and the fact that he had so easily vanquished Secily made him wonder how much higher he could set his sights. He gave her the brush off, and Secily withdrew. Peder had to admit to the sick surge of power that came from subjecting a woman to such a mortifying about-face.

As soon as she was gone, however, his thoughts turned back to his predicament. If he only knew more about *why* Lindon had run the company into the ground, he thought. As feeble an intellectual comfort as that would be, it was the only thing left to him. Yet Zuzanna had not contacted him since their last meeting, so, even if the Mafia had learned anything more about Lindon, they were keeping it to themselves.

Heads up: next incoming was Moinica Mountbatten. Peder had only known Moinica dimly, and she rarely deigned to talk to him. But he noted that the women approaching him were steadily increasing in grade. This was natural intra-sex competitiveness.

He and Moinica proceeded, and again he was surprised by how easily the negotiations went. ... And *again* he concluded them in only 24 lines. But, as before, he decided to stop short. The way he was batting tonight, he would settle for nothing less than the best.

After that thrilling negotiation, it took Peder a full fifteen seconds before he went back to brooding on Lindon. He wanted answers, and, for a moment, he resolved to find them for himself. ... But had he not gone to the Mafia as a way of 'finding out for himself'? And, with that spent, what other options were left to him?

These brooding thoughts were finally abolished, however, when he caught sight of the best of the best: Belinda Goodgrave. Peder first sensed her presence as a prickling sensation. When he spied her, she was lit only slyly by the room's lights, with flirtatious pieces of her body sliding in and out of visibility. This made her so much more the cynosure, to be revealed only in tantalizing fragments. She wore an indigo dress that grasped her curves so jealously that it must have been nanossembled in-place atop her skin. Her moderate bust was transformed into something firm and pertinacious. And her sable hair was done up in a chignon, with a few coquettish curls dangling before her face.

For years, Peder had considered Belinda the aloof, unattainable ideal—his benchmark by which all other women were judged. —And she was steering for *him*, he realized.

He had little time to strategize. Why would Belinda speak to him? ... But word must have reached her that a man was back and shooting down women wildly—and ones previously far above his own grade. Belinda would of course never have heard of this 'Peder Kjaerstad,' but she would have drawn the conclusion that he had either ascended to a whole new tier of wealth, or—as was more likely—he was on the cusp of bankruptcy and was trying to score one more time, as high as he could, before the end. This was a ripe time when a woman could extract more from a man in a few days than she would in months of courting someone far richer.

So that was what Belinda was coming for. She knew he was doomed, but she would offer him the roller coaster ride of his life beforehand—and expect dear payment in return. Yet none of this would come to pass unless Peder could hit an out-of-the-park, grand slam negotiation.

Belinda closed in and said his name, "Peder ... " with a subtle opening leer.

"Belinda ... " he answered with savory, as if reciting the name of a rich dessert.

They took their places on a loveseat.

"And just where have you been all this time?" Belinda asked warmly, her grin full of pouting red lips.

Peder warmed to this manufactured familiarity: her asking 'where have you been' despite the fact that they had never spoken before.

He considered his answer carefully. He rejected several versions in the blink of an eye before he said:

"Surviving."

His delivery had been masterful—flat, forceful, *manly*. The way a soldier back from the Battle of Stalingrad might have described what he had been doing.

"All work and no play?" replied Belinda coyly.

"None at all," Peder made a sly suggestion.

They both centimetered closer to each other.

"You must be starved by now," Belinda gave her head a taunting shake.

Peder leaned in closer. "Ravenous."

And with that he had sealed the deal. Checking his OHUD LifeLog for the tally, he saw it had taken only 6 lines and 25 words. James Bond could not have done better.

***

In the instant immediately after climax, Peder knew he had failed. He should have listened to his inner voice, but no, he had felt no disgrace—until just after he had had what he wanted. Belinda had once been the summit of his earthly desires, but now she was a mirror reflecting back all his failings.

At last it was clear to him. He had thought he had gone to the party in search of pleasure, but here he was barely five seconds past his hookup with Belinda and his thoughts were still drifting back to Lindon and the company. He had been after escape.

Peder had helped Lindon build a private army, and he bore the responsibility for what was done with it. He was responsible for Mohr and Stils and Junge and the hundreds of other men whose fates he had signed over. Yet, despite the company's terminal state, Lindon was still engaged in a master plan: demanding ceasefires, maneuvering his army, orchestrating a strategy ... If he was not resigned to fate, then neither could be Peder.

So he was decided. He would act. He would rebel. And, if Lindon was running a flagship company into the ground to support his schemes, then the least Peder could do was send his own meager net worth augering in alongside. This was his resolution. The only problem was he still had no idea what he could possibly do ...

Correction: that was only one of two problems he faced, the other being how to deal with the goddess who had just curled up beside him on the bed in his 5,000 credit–a–night penthouse suite. Peder had spurned other women that night, but one did not spurn any woman in post-coital circumstances such as these. The finer points of chivalry aside, Peder was also momentarily weakened and drained, which meant that there was a window of opportunity where Belinda—if sufficiently enraged—could feasibly murder him. Best to stay on her good side.

But Peder reasoned that Problem Two could be no more of a challenge than Problem One. And for the moment he decided to sleep on them both.

Chapter 8 - Mistrust

Willoch was sitting in the situation room, her attention riveted on the event clock: +11:55:43—the time since the intercept of the second pirate hypercomm signal. The Hezokeen had been inactive for the last few hours, and the Admirals were overdue to discuss it. But Willoch sensed that they were all waiting for the clock to roll over to +12 hours even before they did so. She wondered whether this were a specifically Human thing—waiting around for place value number systems to align.

At +12:00:05, Lightman was the first to lean forward and say, "Well, I think it's official. We dodged a bullet."

"The Hezokeen aren't going anywhere," Cao affirmed. "Not anywhen soon, at least."

Against her better instincts to paranoia, Willoch had to agree.

"Although I wouldn't really say we 'dodged a bullet'—through any action of our own," she said. "Back when the Hezokeen received the second signal, they could have just charged in, and we weren't ready to fend them off. But instead they embarked on those four hours of hit-and-run attacks on the sensor grid ... "

"Yes, those attacks didn't make much sense to me, either," grumbled Suvorov. "If the Hezokeen had sent out just a few of those sorties it would have looked like they were probing. But they sent out hundreds of those hammer–destroyer groups—and they only destroyed a couple dozen drones. And Hadamard's ships have already deployed enough replacements."

"Exactly." Willoch sighed. "Though ... if Humanity has 'dodged a bullet' at all, I'd say it's how there's been no global panic. We've been staring down a possible alien invasion for the past twelve hours, yet there've been no leaks and no hysteria."

"The markets haven't budged either ... " said Lightman, glancing at the stock ticker he always had open in his OHUD.

"I did see a few articles about the alert, but they weren't too sensational," said Schleicher. "And the typical commentary only ran that it was likely 'more military scaremongering,'" he scoffed.

"Is it time we stood down the fleets?" Cao posed.

"Quite," answered Schleicher. "It's obvious the invasion we feared isn't coming. So ... stand everything down to condition three and ... pull back to inner system orbits? Agreed?"

The room quickly concurred.

"Though let's not park the fleet back at Gateway just yet," Willoch added. "It was no small feat to get everything put out to space. So, while they're there, I think we should be running drills and improving our readiness."

"Absolutely," said Lightman. "We may have gotten everything in the air, but I still feel like we ended up wearing our boots on the wrong feet."

"In fact," said Suvorov, "let's put together a full war game and practice just the odds we'll face in this invasion. Take, say ... a hundred of the ships, with seventy on attack and thirty on defense. We'll place interception in the Öort Cloud just within the Stage One Monitoring Lines ... "

The Admirals were quickly drawn into this construction of a war game.

With the sense of emergency passed, Willoch finally remembered the Home Guard. She had told them to scramble seven hours ago, and they would need stand down orders themselves. She pulled up the original message she had sent announcing the alert and drafted a quick 'all clear' as a follow-up. She would also like to see after action reports from them, but she was afraid what those would look like. The Home Guard was much more poorly organized than her fleet.

Willoch's attention was pulled back to the meeting by something Admiral Cao said:

"... and I'd also be interested in consulting with the Lontan Ambassador as soon as possible."

"Ah yes," said Ibuka. "He may be able to shed some light on what the Hezokeen meant with those hit-and-run attacks."

"Are you sure about that?" Willoch inserted askance, glancing at them without moving her head.

The others looked at her questioningly.

"You can ask the Ambassador about the Hezokeen," Willoch explained, "but how much honesty can you expect from him? In case you forgot, those are his friends out there."

Cao was a moment deciphering this. Then he remembered the suspicions that had been raised by the Zaichi Ambassador: hinting that the Lontan Ambassador had been the source of the leak that had betrayed the Earth's location.

"There's no proof of that," he replied, frowning slightly.

"Oh, of course there's no *proof* of it," Willoch objected, leaning forward. "I don't doubt that, if the Lontan Ambassador wanted to double-cross us, he could do so without leaving behind any evidence that we could detect. But it still stands that he most likely sold out our trade route to these pirates himself."

"That's still a stretch for me, Lene," said Lightman.

"And I," added Schleicher.

Willoch looked around, flustered. She had been cultivating these suspicions about the Ambassador for so long that she had expected to find ready sympathy when she at last gave them voice. Now realizing that no one shared her apprehensions, they all seemed credulous sheep.

"When are we going to stop blindly trusting the Lontans?" she insisted. "For all we know, the Ambassador could be responsible for so much more than just tipping the Hezokeen off to our location.

He was the one, after all, who first suggested that tithing option. Maybe he only did so because he knew the Hezokeen would steal all of our ships, and he was set to profit by it."

"You recommended that tithing option yourself, Lene," said Schleicher, trying to steal her thunder.

"Yes, I did—which is why you should take this accusation coming from me so seriously."

He cocked his head in a shrug.

Willoch needed more fodder to continue her argument. She scrounged for any evidence of a Lontan deception, no matter how circumstantial.

"Think about these intercepted hypercomm signals—the ones from the Hezokeen's terrestrial agents. —*Or so they say*. Our own equipment can't pin down the source, so we have to rely on the information the Ambassador is feeding us through the Embassy. And the Lontans claim that the signals are coming from somewhere Earth-side, but how do we know they weren't sent from somewhere else? Maybe even from the Embassy itself? ... Maybe even by the *Ambassador* himself?"

Willoch saw the plain disbelief on the others' faces.

"Okay, even I don't believe the Ambassador's gone *that* far ... " she admitted. "But think about how exposed it leaves us to trust the Lontans completely."

"You have a good point, Lene," said Suvorov. "But, still, what can it hurt to consult with the Ambassador? As long as we know to take what he says with healthy suspicion, then it can actually give us more information than not."

"And what other option is there?" asked Lightman. "To stonewall the Ambassador and refuse to meet with him at all? But that would be suspicious. Especially since this action from the Hezokeen is something we would discuss with him at any other time."

He left a space for Willoch to respond, but she stayed silent.

"I'm not saying that we shouldn't be maintaining any suspicions about the Lontans," he continued. "Hell, I agree with you that the Ambassador has built up some damned peculiar circumstances around himself concerning these pirates. But, while we're doing that, let's not be so foolish as to advertise our suspicions to the people we suspect. Let's play it cool."

Willoch gave a begrudged nod. They were right, and she had only made her original outburst as a way of seeking sympathy. She would have gone to meet with the Ambassador no matter what, if only for appearances. The issue was dropped.

But soon after Willoch realized—with a nervous pang—that this was the first time she and the Admirals had ever openly discussed any mistrust of the Lontans. That alone struck her as foolhardy. Lightman had said it was unwise to advertise their suspicions, but, considering the Lontans' million-year technological lead, how did Humanity know it could keep any secrets from them? Even in their own thoughts? Willoch could meet with the Ambassador to keep up a polite facade, but whom would she be fooling?

Chapter 9 - Intuition

Frisch was in the *Jotunheim's* mess, a now cold meal sitting untouched before him. His hands clutched a knife and fork but his arms were resting on the table, merely surrounding the plate in a lackadaisical siege. Frisch's attention was engaged not in his food but in the holodisplay swirling above it, alive with tactical replays of the Hezokeen attacks on the sensor grid.

The general feeling around the fleet was one of relief: a Hezokeen invasion had not materialized, and the aliens had blundered with their probing attacks on the sensor grid. Before this the Hezokeen had been a great, faceless foe, made ten times worse by the Humans' blind estimation. But now Human morale was up. Which was why Frisch—as a self-anointed counterweight—had sunk into this quandary.

If he had to paraphrase the suspicion circling his mind, it would go, 'Never underestimate your enemy. Nor should you, when the enemy hands you an estimation of themselves, take it at face value.' I.e., the Hezokeen had looked so stupid with their attacks that the only explanation was that they must have been trying to look stupid. Otherwise, how could a species that dumb even survive? The universe was not like it was in the vids, where aliens could be idiot savants who had invented warp drives and teleporters while overstepping basic intelligence.

There had to be an explanation for why the Hezokeen were trying to look stupid. The most obvious one was that they were trying to make the Humans feel over-confident, but that was too simple. Frisch sensed that there had to be something deeper. The only thing smarter than doing something smart was disguising it as something that looked stupid—the queen sacrifice in chess, say. Meanwhile those Hezokeen attacks on the grid had looked positively asinine, so they had to be masking some hidden genius of commensurate scale.

Frisch wanted to share these suspicions with someone, but alas one could not go up the chain of command with just uneasy feelings and apt quotations from *The Art of War*. One needed evidence, proof. Which was why he was re-watching the fleet actions: to find out what he had missed—what they had all missed. Yet, despite staring at the replays for an hour, he had nothing.

He got up from the mess table and walked down to the rec room. There he saw Kittelsen and Diesen playing darts, Evensen and Koltsov at the pool table, and Riiser bent over a book. Then Frisch realized that, while one could not go *up* the chain of command with vague feelings and nebulous objectives, those were just the things that flowed *down* that apparatus like running water.

"I've got an assignment for you," he said, drawing the room's attention. He explained his suspicions, described what he was looking for, and showed them what he had examined in the replays.

After all his hand-waving, Kittelsen asked, "So, what *exactly* are we looking for, sir?"

"Nothing 'exact,'" answered Frisch. "Just anything. Anything hidden, suggestive, or deceptive."

Chapter 10 - Deal

Zuzanna was sitting at her ASAPR desk, the wallscreen alight with the image of her boss, Mikhi Takacs. They were wrapping up a meeting and Mikhi's head was bent down as he read through some notes. Meanwhile he was tracing his fingers along his pencil-thin beard, and also tousling the chest hair that peeked out through his shirt neck. Zuzanna detested these quirks, but, whenever Mikhi caught her averting her eyes, he would redouble them. Zuzanna imagined this was why their bosses had assigned her to him: he inflicted upon her a constant low level of torture, thus reminding her of what was the Mafia's main disciplinary tool.

"Sooo ... " said Mikhi after a long pause, "you want the Tanjin-Cambarran job?"

Zuzanna recalled the details: Malaysian work, mid-level corporate, moderate danger—as such things went.

"I'd have to move a lot of resources down to Indochina ... " she said.

"And?" Mikhi objected. "They say that's where the recovery's going to start."

Zuzanna eyed him. "I didn't know that the long-awaited 'recovery' had started anywhere."

"Of course it hasn't, but it might as well start in Asia as anywhere—newest economies, highest population densities ... But you've looked over the file, so do you want the job or not?"

"Is there no other team that would like it?"

Mikhi's face darkened.

"—I know we're not supposed to turn down anything reasonable, so, if it comes to that, I'll take it. But this would throw my unit all off-keel. There's gotta be another team that's better able to—"

"Zuzanna Arkadyevna," Mikhi scolded her, using her patronymic. "You should be happy I'm coming to you with this first. You set us up for a nice profit on the Lindon job, and I thought I'd reward you by giving you the lead on the next big one."

Zuzanna inhaled deeply and held her breath—a reverse sigh. "Of course. I'll take it. Just give me a week to gear up."

"Three days," Mikhi smiled, flashing a glimpse of his gold-and-diamond teeth.

"Is that it?"

Mikhi nodded. "*Da*. Go get 'em, Zizi."

Zuzanna closed the channel—and cursed Mikhi's image as it disappeared. The man made more money on her jobs than she did.

She logged off her computer. She had a great deal of work to do, but her meetings with Mikhi always left her with a deep need for palate cleansing. So she picked up the watering pitcher beside her desk and began tending to her plants. She worked her way around the ASAPR, following a precise order. As she watched the water arc out of the stippled holes in the pitcher's spout, she tried to

71

imagine tension and anxiety flowing out of herself along mirror trajectories.

This was how she usually eliminated stress. It had even become a ritual for her to head down to her ASAPR with the pitcher full, so that it would be ready for her immediately after her calls. She could get a good barometric reading on her mood just by counting how many pitchers it took her before she felt well enough to return to work.

"Excuse me," came a voice from behind her.

The pitcher leapt out of Zuzanna's hands and she grabbed the potted plant she had been watering as a makeshift weapon. She whirled around to see a man sitting in her ASAPR.

"—Pardon the intrusion," he said again, and this time Zuzanna noted his English accent.

But this was impossible! she thought. The ASAPR should never have permitted an unauthorized entry, and it would have at least told her if someone had broken in ... This could only mean that the man was a vizhack—something rendered on Zuzanna's comps for her eyes only. But she ran some internal security sweeps and found none of the usual telltales.

"Allow me to introduce myself: Special Agent Townsend, ISSO." The man held up his hand and flashed a holo ID.

The incursion of an ISSO agent into Zuzanna's sanctum should have been awful, but this was actually the best possible turn of events. Had any of the Mafia's competitors acquired such an ability, they would have used it to assassinate her organization, and Zuzanna would have been dead as of five seconds ago. But the worst the feds would likely do was talk to her.

Zuzanna tamped down on her fight reflex. She righted the pitcher on the floor, set down the potted plant she had grabbed, and smoothed its upset dirt. She grimaced at her defensive reflex. She tended to her plants like children, but, when in danger, had she not picked up one of her 'children' to use as a missile?

"How did you get in here?" she finally challenged the man.

"And you are Zuzanna Mukhina," he continued obliviously, "a Mafia sleuth attached to Scandinavia—and first-class, I hear. Pleased to meet you."

"Yes, delighted—Now how the *hell* did you get in here?"

"Not by any means you're thinking. I'm actually in the Stockholm ISSO office, and what you're seeing is a projected hologram."

Zuzanna's eyes went wide—that was impossible on so many counts. The longest-range holoprojection she had ever heard of was only over fifty meters. —And then it was impossible to project anything inside of an ASAPR anyway. She tried to mouth several eloquent objections, but all that came out was:

"Wha—Why—How—It— ... Th—That's impossible!"

"True, we're inside of an ASAPR and that should be impossible. But think what 'ASAPR' means: 'As Secure As Possible' *for Humans*. And, right now, I'm not using Human technology."

"... The Lontans."

Townsend nodded. "They're working with us on a case. And availing us of their far superior abilities, as you can see. I just had to wait until you were alone in your ASAPR to contact you. Not that the technology *I'm* using requires it, but I still wanted this to be as secure as possible from your end."

The man's hologram was seated in one of her ASAPR's chairs, so she calmly took the one opposite him. Business-like, she crossed her legs and smoothed out her dress. But she maintained a hostile tone when she asked,

"Well? What is this about?"

"Lindon Securities," said Townsend, steepling his hands. "We know you conducted an investigation into them on behalf of Peder Kjaerstad. And that you discovered some interesting things in the process. What we want—"

"Hold it. I don't deal with feds. Nor anyone besides paying customers. You know who I work for, so obviously you must know *that*."

"Oh, don't worry, we're not asking you to betray your bosses—not asking you to betray *any* of your people, in fact. We just want the information you collected on Lindon, and then maybe a favor or two afterwards. And, as for payment, I thought my identity should make it plain enough what I'm offering."

A deal, she knew. But, "Bullshit," she retorted. "The Human authorities couldn't have anything on us, so whatever you have is probably all thanks to the Lontans—like this fancy projection rig here. And, without an explicit prior warrant, that kind of evidence is inadmissible in a Human court."

Townsend nodded at her spirit. Evidently the Mafia covered itself from every legal angle imaginable, including possible alien intervention. Even with the Lontan Governate come knocking at her door, Mukhina could stand in defiant resolve.

"Okay, I'll give you that one, we can't put you in jail. But I *can* push on two dozen other ISSO and local police investigations into your organization. You may have run a tight operation yourself, but not all your coworkers are so careful. The evidence is weak, but I could have twenty Mafia operatives scooped up in an hour, and then a hundred more by the end of the day.

"Then we start grilling them all on what do they know about this 'Zuzanna Mukhina' and some operations we think she's running on the side. I kick a few out on bail, and they go running back to their bosses with your name fresh on their minds. So now your bosses think you're responsible for getting half their intel organization scooped up, and that you're two-timing them.

"Now, if that's a situation that you think you can dig yourself out of perfectly unscathed, then, hey, more power to you. Me and the Lontans will go fuck ourselves, and you can have a nice day."

Zuzanna stared back murderously, vying with Townsend on the unspoken battlefield of poker faces and sangfroid.

"*Or*," Townsend turned, "I can offer you immunity for everything up to and including the conclusion of your cooperation with us. Now I'm just guessing here, but that's probably a deal worth about five hundred years of prison time."

Zuzanna frowned as she considered his offer. To betray the Mafia to the ISSO carried with it consequences that were beyond medieval. Torture had entered a golden age as recently as the invention of the chainsaw, and that golden age had gone into overtime thanks to the blowtorch, rap music, and nanocomposters.

Weighing the options, she thought positively that Townsend was not asking her to betray the Mafia *itself*, only information they had gathered on another company. At worst that might do peripheral damage by revealing their information collection methods, but it would not seriously harm the organization. If her bosses ever found out about this, they might even forgive her, since this compromise had ended up keeping a hundred of their people out of jail. If only she could get a receipt from the ISSO to that effect ...

Once she finished tallying the points, her choice seemed between 'terrible pain and certain death now' and 'significant probability of the same later.' Curse the feds and their deals ...

"All right," she cut.

"Good. So, first things first, I need everything you got from your investigations into Lindon's company."

"Don't you have that already? I thought the Lontans were working with you."

"Well, yes, the Lontans could have collected this information just by eavesdropping on you back when *you* got it, but they weren't doing that back then. So, if you don't mind ... "

Zuzanna rummaged around in her OHUD. "Uh, how do I send it to you—"

"Just put it into a public space, please—ah, there, we've got it."

"... And now you mentioned a favor?"

"Ah, not so fast. I said to give us *everything* you recovered, and, while we may not *have* what you have, we do *know* what you have. So we know what you're holding out on."

Zuzanna smirked. She had withheld some data not because she had anything to hide but because it was a simple reflex. The feds had forced her compliance, so naturally she was going to make her cooperation as stingy and refractory as possible.

"Do you have a Lontan over there right now, whispering over your shoulder?" she asked.

"Just about."

Zuzanna made a second transfer, but she kept this one incomplete, as well. She was curious as to whether Townsend really could tell when she was holding out, since his demanding more information might simply have been as natural a reflex as her withholding it.

After receiving her second burst, Townsend cleared his throat. "Thank you, but I wasn't bluffing: we *really do* know how much you have. So either you send over everything now, or the deal's off. This is the last time I'll let you try and play us for fools."

More than threatened, Zuzanna was pleasantly surprised at this display of the ISSO's abilities. Law enforcement intervened so rarely in her world that she had come to think it was because they were outclassed. But this made her see the ISSO more like an adult stepping into a playground squabble.

She made a last, complete transfer to Townsend.

"Ah, splendid," the agent said. "And the next thing we need is ... here." A holo appeared next to him. Zuzanna recognized it as part of the payroll database she had just transferred. Several entries were highlighted with contact IPs and bank accounts.

"We find these names to be of interest. Contact them, arrange a meeting as soon as you can, and collect any information on their associations with Lindon."

Zuzanna grimaced. "Why can't the ISSO—or the *Lontans*—do that themselves?"

"That should be obvious. These are the kind of people who can see feds coming a klick away. So instead we get some trustworthily shady figure— like yourself—to make contact for us while we sit back and watch it unfold."

Zuzanna huffed. "Okay. But I heard you right: immunity?"

"Yes."

"—And I want immunity from the Lontans, too, and whatever evidence they may have collected."

"Oh, don't worry, you'll get retroactive immunity, a signed get-out-of-jail-free card, a fuckbarge orbiting Jupiter if you want it."

"Fine."

"Just don't waste time. Because, for every second you keep me waiting, I'm only collecting more evidence on *you*, and that immunity deal only kicks in *after* you've made me happy. Clear?"

Zuzanna nodded sensibly. "Clear."

"It's been a pleasure doing business with you."

"Not at all likewise."

Townsend grinned. "Good day, Mizz Mukhina."

"Mister Townsend," she said, using his name for the first time.

The man's holo abruptly disappeared, and Zuzanna found herself alone.

Chapter 11 - Overhaul

The last good night's sleep Willoch had had was down on Earth, thirty-seven hours ago, and since then she had stayed awake only by surfing atop narcotic doses of caffeine. But her mind's weariness was becoming overpowering. Back in the situation, several times she had 'woken up' while finding herself in the middle of saying something she could not remember. She could only assume that her brain had briefly managed the dolphin-like feat of sleeping in one hemisphere while the other kept a hand on the wheel. She was now back in her quarters and could rest, but so much work pressed in on her that that was unthinkable. So she fixed herself some coffee, some espresso, and even brought out her *cafetiere à piston*. Then she settled in at her desk.

First on her agenda was to look through the after action reports she had received from the Home Guard commanders on their cities' drills. Every city had sent back a report—except for Bergen. That city had not even run a drill at all. This irked Willoch. Granted she no longer had any real authority over the Home Guard—she had only 'suggested' that they run a drill in the first place. Yet everyone had taken her seriously ... except for Bergen's Colonel Brechts. He had replied only to acknowledge her warning, to assure her that Bergen's units were up to any challenge, and to thank her in advance for alerting them in case a true emergency ever did develop.

"Jackass," she said aloud, re-reading his words. And she laughed—everything seemed funny after being awake for two days.

But Willoch really did not need to see a report from Bergen. The other cities' performance had all been so dismal that she could easily extrapolate how horrendous Bergen's would have been. She had asked for 'disaster response' and instead gotten seven hours of raucous parody thereof. Willoch knew that the Home Guard had to overhaul its evacuation strategies, build and stock enough fallout shelters to house millions, and ramrod through a crash course in disaster preparedness. Yet, while the cities had obeyed her suggestion to conduct a drill, less eager would they be to sink millions of credits they did not have into building fallout shelters they would not think they needed. Willoch would have to go to all the mayors and manhandle them one-by-one to get anything done, but she had no time to spare from the fleet right now.

Luckily, she was personal friends with a respected Norwegian mayor who would be the perfect busybody-by-proxy to effect all this. She had to check the clock to make sure it was a sane hour down in Norway, but then she placed a call to Mayor Jakob Laurantzson. The channel connected a minute later, showing Laurantzson in his office, basking in midday light.

"Ah, Lene," the man greeted her. After some pleasantries, he added, a little urgently, "So ... it appears you had a situation up there yesterday?"

Willoch then realized what yesterday's alert would have looked like from Laurantzson's perspective. First, emergency agencies the world over going into a panic; second, the black-water fleets scrambling; third, ominous rumors leaking down from Gateway Station; and finally, a cryptic message from Willoch that sent the Home Guard into a fit. To him, the fact that the world had still been in one piece this morning had probably not been a trivial observation.

"Yes, a 'situation,'" Willoch replied delicately. "I shouldn't reveal too many specifics, but ... for a while we were afraid that the Hezokeen fleet was going to attack."

Willoch expected some wide-eyed reaction from him, but she instead received a searching glance and:

"The Hezo— ... Hezo— ... Hezo—who did you say?"

Now Willoch became wide-eyed. "*The Hezokeen pirate fleet.* I briefed you on them before."

Laurantzson was finally struck with recollection. "Ah, yes. ... Indeed. ... Oh! And an invasion you say?"

"Yes," Willoch shifted in her seat, stifling her urge to remonstrate. "Luckily the danger seems passed—for the moment. But that was why I wanted the Home Guard and the other agencies running disaster drills. That way, if the Hezokeen invaded and we needed to prepare for planetary bombardment, at least we'd have a head start."

Laurantzson nodded slowly. He looked to be still digesting the weightier words in Willoch's last sentence: 'invaded,' 'bombardment,' etc. At last he replied,

"Then I must thank and commend you for ordering that drill. It was exactly the response needed. I disliked how Brechts shirked it off, and, now knowing the reason behind it, I must say that he acted negligently. But, by the time I'd heard about your message, you had already sent your 'stand down' and it hardly seemed productive for me to countermand him."

"Thank ... you," Willoch replied—a delicately complex answer given the number of ideas she could have been replying to. "And now, Jakob, I need your help to take the next step.

"I asked the Home Guard and other agencies to scramble, and they did, but their overall performance was very poor. If an invasion comes, the best we can do is get everyone out of the cities, but that's not saying much—fleeing in a panicked mob doesn't take much choreography. So ... " She trailed off, having forgotten what she wanted to say. After this much sleep deprivation, her train of thought was as slippery as an eel. "— So every agency needs to conduct a complete overhaul of its plans. We need new evacuation routes, new emergency plans, and fallout and impact shelters constructed. And we need this to happen as soon as possible. Significant headway by the end of the week at the latest."

Laurantzson had felt he had been taking this alert seriously enough, but he balked at this prescription.

"Is it really so grave as all that, Lene?" He made a show of placing his tea cup back on its saucer and setting it far away on his desk, as if Willoch had spoiled his tea-drinking mood.

"*Yes*sss,"—she tried not to over-stress and failed, then slid back to a more neutral tone. "Even if we get everyone out of the cities, they'd still just be above ground and out in the open. The only way they'd be safe is if the Hezokeen just lobbed down a few Megaton nukes blindly and the fallout drifted nowhere harmful. But... "—thought hiccup—"but there are modern weapons that, if detonated anywhere inside of the *moon's orbit*, would kill everyone on Earth not in a hardened structure."

"I don't doubt what would be the seriousness of such an attack, Lene. But do you really believe one is imminent?"

Willoch suppressed a sigh. "I pray one is not. But the Hezokeen have given us no reason to discount an invasion, so we have to prepare for it. If so much as one stray warhead gets down here, we are going to have a disaster and loss of life at least on the scale of the Singularity, and likely worse."

84

Laurantzson drew back in contemplation. His hand wandered back over to his teacup and he began turning it around in place on its saucer. At length he flicked a fingernail into its handle, exciting a bright *ting* that Willoch heard over the commline.

"Then I suppose ... you are right, Lene," he said, a little sullenly. "And this truce with Lindon might give us just the opportunity to do as you ask. —Of course we'll need to keep enough Home Guard units in place to watch over the corporate army's withdrawal. But the balance of them could be put to this task immediately."

"Thank you, Jakob."

Their call was finished soon after.

Willoch had won the concession she wanted, but Laurantzson's hesitancy told her that nothing would come of it—at least not as quickly as she needed it to. If she wanted change, she would have to appeal to an even higher power ...

Towards that end, she thought of the meeting she had coming up with the Lontan Ambassador. Before this she had only been thinking of how distasteful it would be to meet with him, but now she realized there was a favor she could ask.

Laiidjokun and Goldam were right about the Lontans' doctrine of fairness: they never did Humanity any favors unless those favors were benign and uniformly distributed. But, so long as one knew the formula, it should be easy to frame something to their liking. She could ask the Lontans to build these fallout shelters themselves, or at least supply every government with the proper construction kits. Willoch only needed to couch her request in the right terms—throw in that 'international' buzzword enough times.

Willoch refilled her coffee and went about scripting her request for the Ambassador. At times she had stumbled for words while talking to Laurantzson because of her weariness, but she was determined to present the Ambassador with her usual polished mien.

Chapter 12 - Discovery

Frisch was at one of the side exits of the crew capsule, waiting for the ship to finish building his running course. The crew capsule was the only permanently habitable section of the ship, but the *Jotunheim* itself was really a giant nanossembler, so it could build any facility for them on demand. Gyms and exercise tracks were what the crew prevailed on this ability the most for, and Frisch had just dialed up his *2001: A Space Odyssey*–style hamster wheel running course.

Just as the construction finished, someone came vaulting up the stairway. "Ah, Captain," said Khlebnikova, "glad I caught you before you went out."

"Anything wrong?" Frisch turned to her with concern—and he was already checking ship status in his OHUD.

"—No—no," she said quickly. "It's just that Sonja has a theory about the Hezokeen deception that you had the crew looking for."

Frisch was not immediately impressed. He had spent the last five hours down in the rec room bouncing dead end theories off the crew and having them bounced off him. He was going running to take a break. ... But he did recall seeing Sonja working off by herself most of the time, so perhaps she had a fresh take.

"Is it worth anything?" he asked.

Khlebnikova shrugged. "Haven't seen it yet myself, but Riiser says it's good. If you came down, she could run it by the rest of the crew."

Frisch acceded, and moved downstairs.

Seven of his crew were gathered around the main table. All were seated except Sonja Diesen, who stood before them in front of a vidscreen, ready to give her presentation. She appeared fidgety, but Frisch did not think this was from nervousness— they all knew each other too well. Was she anxious? Excited?

"Captain," they greeted him. Frisch and Khlebnikova took their seats in front.

"So you've got something," Frisch entreated her.

"Indeed, sir," Diesen chirped. "So, Captain, you told us to look for anything suspicious in the Hezokeen's actions. I chased that around for a few hours—like most everyone else—, but didn't find anything. And after a while I admitted that maybe looking for 'anything' was a hopelessly large task— where do you start? So I thought about taking a different approach. Maybe we should try and figure out what the Hezokeen might have liked to hide *first*, then go back and look for evidence of *that*. Kind of Bayes Rule'ing the approach."

"I follow you," said Frisch—and was amazed that he actually did where Bayesian analogies were involved.

"So I asked myself what could the Hezokeen have wanted to hide with this attack on the grid. We

88

were all looking for an ulterior motive, like using this fake attack to mask something else. But after a while I thought maybe there wasn't an 'ulterior' motive like we were expecting. Maybe the Hezokeen *really were* trying to destroy the sensor grid. Only they made this first show of doing it poorly because they were really setting the stage to destroy it later intelligently."

"Hm," Frisch mumbled positively. "I like it. A typical deception is you're trying to use A to distract from B. But here you're suggesting the Hezokeen used A to distract from a different way of getting A—call it A'. ... That's even more obfuscated than I was thinking."

"Thank you, sir." Sonja proceeded, "So, if the Hez were trying to destroy the sensor grid, there were a few tactics that worked best. Such as this."

She played a tactical clip on the holo. It was a maneuver they were all familiar with: a Hezokeen hammer–destroyer group punched through to the outside of the sensor grid and shot off into the deep field, out of range of the grid's sensors. Minutes later the group looped back, charging a different, random section of the grid. Simultaneously a Hezokeen group on the inside would push outwards, and the two would catch a large swath of probes in a pincer move. Most of the probes still escaped, but these maneuvers had netted the Hezokeen their only kills.

Sonja explained: "Their best strategy was to get some ships outside of the grid, then have them re-attack in tandem with those on the inside. It had promise ... but the problem was the Hezokeen never put enough ships into these maneuvers to be effective. Here they used a half-dozen ships on either side and they only trapped a handful of probes.

"But what if the Hezokeen had duplicated this maneuver using twenty ships? Fifty ships? A hundred? If they could sneak *that* many ships outside of the grid and coordinate an attack, then this pincer move could take out a huge swath of the grid. Then, before we could rebuild it, the Hezokeen fleet could disappear through the gap."

Frisch shrugged. "Okay. But when did they sneak a hundred ships outside of the grid?"

"Right, sir. The grid was watching them the whole time, so how did they get any ships out? So I looked again at the hammer attacks they ran on our probes.

"We all thought the purpose of those maneuvers was for the hammers to mask the destroyers as they pushed in on our probes. But what if they were using the hammers for something else, too? Because, generally, what is it that hammers do?" She paused to indicate a coming epiphany. "They create *blind spots*."

She had put a great deal of emphasis into this word choice, but Frisch and the others were not struck by it. She tried again:

"What if the Hezokeen weren't just using the hammers to obscure the movements of those destroyers? What if they were using them to keep us from seeing other ships, too? A small group that was tagging along with the hammers—unseen—the entire time? And the destroyers' pointless attacks were only meant to distract us from this?"

Frisch paused to consider ... and nodded tepidly. So far this was the most promising—and longest-lived—pitch he had heard.

"So I went to the computer and gave it a bunch of these sensor tracks where the Hezokeen groups had broken all the way through to the outside of the grid. I had the comps calculate all of the blind spots that the hammer strokes created in our sensor net, and I had them follow these through time, seeing if they allowed a persistent blind spot to shadow the group. And it turns out ... that nearly *half* of the Hezokeen groups had one of these. Some of them were even big enough to hide ten ships in."

She brought up some figures on the holo: time-condensed projections of several Hezokeen groups' paths through the sensor grid. The persistent blind spots were drawn in, appearing as red, globular regions that shadowed the groups all along the way. It was an underground railroad for Hezokeen ships to escape undetected.

"Nice discovery," commented Khlebnikova. "But just showing that there were these persistent blind spots doesn't mean that the Hezokeen actually used them to sneak their ships out. These blind spots might have just been accidental. They might even have been a statistical eventuality given how much the Hez were spamming with those hammers."

"Granted, ma'am," said Sonja. "All I've shown is that they could have done it, but how to prove that they actually did? So I thought, even if these Hez ships were hidden from our direct sensor visibility, we might still be able to detect them from the one thing that all ships put out. A wake."

"Whoa whoa whoa," Koltsov jumped in. "A ship's hyperwake is too weak compared to a hammer stroke. It would have been washed out of these sensor readings."

"Not entirely, there should always be some residual. And look at this."

She brought up a sensor log freeze frame. It showed a sphere of hypernoise surrounding a Hezokeen hammer, plus a flight of destroyers lancing outwards. Into this frame she inserted the blind spot that had been extrapolated by the computer.

"This," she pointed at the red region, "is the blind spot where the hidden ships would have been. So we should be seeing a roughly conical wake behind it, here." She traced her fingers out where she meant. "But we don't because the hammer strokes are saturating the display. So I had the computer subtract out their effects."

The sensor data was washed to remove the spherical turbulence, and behind it resolved faintly the wakes of the other ships. But the readings were almost useless: hovering just above the noise floor, they were likely nothing but hiccups in the background static.

"They're very faint," continued Sonja, "so I sharpened them by running a reconstruction algorithm—something that would take all the small sensor blips and try to explain them by saying, 'Here's a ship,' 'There's a ship.'"

"You should know that you can't run a reconstruction algorithm on this data," Koltsov said. "You already subtracted out most of the signal with the hammer stroke, so all you have left is the dither. The reconstruction would only return junk."

"Junk, yes, but there should also be some good data thrown in," she countered with alacrity. "Even though most of the signal is noise, some of it isn't, and that's what I'm looking for."

"Thin ice ... " warned Koltsov.

"Let's just look at the results."

The image changed and crystallized. Out of the background static, a series of wakes was identified, and a conjectured ship was drawn behind each. While some of the posited ships did roughly align with actual ships in the display, many of them were erroneous, hovering out in empty space or pitched at unrealistic angles.

"Obviously there are a lot of bogus wakes in here," said Sonja. "So I wrote a few heuristics to throw away any that were too small, too eccentric—"

"Getting thinner ... " said Koltsov.

"I know, I know ... "

The display was cleared of most of the wakes, leaving behind only those that were pitched in sensible directions and that appeared at realistic scales.

"And then I removed all the wakes that could be explained by the known ships."

In turn, the display highlighted the locations of the hammers, destroyers, and corvettes. Only a third of these had had wakes detected around them by Sonja's algorithm, and they were removed. Left behind was a flat volume of hyperspace with just one wake remaining: the faintest of them all, unexplained and emanating from the blind spot.

Frisch shrugged. "Nice, but, as Koltsov pointed out, by now your detection method is like doing a Tarot reading on white noise. Most likely you just got lucky and ended up detecting a wake-shaped seizure in hyperspace right where you wanted it to be."

"That's true, sir. This method recovered a lot of false positives and false negatives, so even hitting the blind spot dead on here was probably just luck. And I ran this exact same procedure on sensor stills from a little before and a little after this frame here, and I couldn't recover the same wake around the blind spot."

"There you go," said Koltsov.

"So I ran this procedure over an *entire* sensor sequence," she countered. "I took a Hez group just as it appeared on the inside of the grid and followed it all the way to the outside—over a hundred

94

seconds of vidage. Now, if this blind spot wake was just a fluke, then it shouldn't appear more often than any other random wake. But, if there really was a ship there, then, even though we might not detect it all of the time, it should still be a salient feature. In other words, we would see *this*:"

The display showed a time-lapsed replay of a Hezokeen group's path through the sensor grid. This was Sonja's processed view of the scene, overlaid with both the group's blind spot and all of the unexplained wakes from her reconstruction. With the vid playing at high speed, most of the wakes returned by her algorithm blinked in and out, spun wildly, and swelled in size such that they could belong to no physical ship. Except for one: hovering around the blind spot was a faint but persistent wake. It appeared intermittently as from a ghost ship, but it was always holding course and speed with the rest of the Hezokeen group. All the way from the inside out.

Now Frisch leaned forward in astonishment. "Play it again," he said.

After the second time through, even Koltsov was nodding.

Sonja went on: "Detecting this blind spot wake just a few times would have been a fluke, but I found it in over a quarter of the sensor stills on these runs. And I ran this processing on other sensor sequences and got similar results.

"So I asked the computer to put a confidence on this. 'Given all of the observed data, what is the

95

probability that these wakes were caused by a ship versus not a ship.' And the answer was ... " She paused and brought the number up on its own slide in her presentation: "82%."

Frisch was pleased with that number. The inner loop of Sonja's algorithm was so fuzzy that he would have been suspicious if the probability had come back too high. But 82% was a good, Human probability, and it felt on par with his own mental level of conviction.

"Can you tell how many ships are in each blind spot?" Frisch asked.

"No, the wakes are too faint," said Sonja disappointedly. "All we can say is that *something's* there."

"How many of these blind spot runs did you detect wakes for?"

"Ninety-five."

Khlebnikova frowned. "If each of those runs held anything more than one ship apiece, we're in trouble ... "

Frisch nodded gravely, knowing the full implications. But he was also thrilled, because this was exactly the ingenious type of move he had expected from the Hezokeen.

"Excellent work," he said.

"Thank you, sir," Sonja glowed. "And I also took the liberty of putting together a draft intelligence product. In case you want to send this up the chain of command ... "

"Oh, definitely. Send it over and we'll take a look."

Sonja obliged, and Frisch and Khlebnikova paged through the document. They found all the same evidence convincingly presented. But, when Frisch reached Sonja's analysis and conclusion section, he noticed a glaring flaw. He glanced at Khlebnikova, and she mirrored his look.

Sonja leaned in nervously. "Is there something wrong, sirs?"

"Your analysis is fine," said Khlebnikova, "but, when you extrapolated to what it meant, you missed the point."

Sonja looked at them quizzically. "But ... that was what I proved—that the Hezokeen snuck a task force out to prepare a large pincer attack. So that they can destroy the sensor grid."

"That may be how you *approached* it, but that's not what you ended up proving. Think about it: if the Hezokeen snuck just one ship out with each blind spot, then they exfiltrated a hundred ships. If they snuck out anything more than one ship at a time, then that number becomes hun*dreds*. So the balance of their fleet could be gone, which would leave no one on the inside to complete the pincer attack.

"And then, if the Hezokeen have several hundred ships running free out there, why do they even need to come back and destroy the sensor grid? They've already circumvented it. In fact, they should leave us alone so that we keep telling Fleet everything's fine and that the Hezokeen haven't moved. Meanwhile they could be hovering right outside of the Monitoring Lines where they could attack *the system* at will. ... *That* was what they were after."

Sonja was struck. This was a clear lesson in hubris. She had been so dazzled by the brilliance of her analysis that she had stumbled into this even more brilliant oversight. She *had* proved that the enemy fleet was on the loose, but her report had only speculated on when that fleet might deviously return to port, and had neglected to imagine any Pearl Harbor-ian escapades that they might indulge in in between.

"Good ... point," she observed, flipping through the document. Seconds ago she had been proud of it; now she could hardly bear to look at the thing. "I've got some rewriting to do."

Chapter 13 - Agenda

Peder sat back down at his ASAPR desk, ready to place his next call. He opened a line to the acquisitions arm of Zuzanna's organization. He drummed his fingers nervously as he waited for the secure line to connect. This was the first concrete step in his counterattack against Lindon.

When the call finally opened, the video came through as white noise but the audio was clear:

"Peder Kjaerstad – ID confirmed – receiving." The voice had been flattened and masked into monotone.

"Afternoon," Peder replied. In an echo channel he heard how his own voice sounded in transmission: squashed down into the same, sterilized rendering as he was speaking to. It was simple prudence not to let his unaltered voice be recorded making a negotiation for illegal goods.

"Your request?" the voice asked.

"I need a commline. Something special."

"What's so special about a commline?"

"It has to have ... penetration."

Peder was proud of how he had solved the problem of just how to 'counterattack' Lindon without even vaguely knowing the man's plans. His inspiration had come from how Lindon had cut contact between him and his men back when he had surrendered control—the same as had happened to all the other corporate army CEOs. Now, while that did not reveal what Lindon was planning, it did say that he wanted no one to be able to contact their men and potentially discover it. So the obvious countermeasure was to break through that isolation, and Peder needed to reestablish communications with his men.

"What kind of penetration?"

"Into a hardened installation. Something opaque to EM."

"Is this typical Faraday cage or something more exotic?"

"Uh ... on the exotic side."

He was being coy for a reason. He needed to communicate with his men while they were inside of the Bunker, the corporate army superbase in Oslo. This was proofed against all forms of Human communication, so Peder needed to purchase black market alien comms tech from the Mafia. Yet he could not just tell them that he needed to crack into the Bunker because that information could be leaked. And neither could he say he needed to crack into a structure with features X, Y, and Z, because the Bunker's characteristics were unique. So he had to delicately steer the negotiation to where he needed.

"What specs can you give me?" the voice asked.

"I don't know exactly, but it's military-grade shielding. A mix of smuggled alien materials that's opaque to all Human comms. It's like the equivalent of Fari torride—meters of it."

There was a slight pause. "Sounds like we could do this with a drift EP."

"No, no, I've tried that. Drift EP won't work."

"... How the fuck did you *try* a drift EP transmitter? 'Cause you sure as fuck didn't get it from us." The voice knew Kjaerstad had an exclusivity deal with the Mafia.

"I mean I *looked into it*," Peder clarified. "This place has got countermeasures against drift EP. That's out."

There was an impatient, disgruntled sound on the line—or what Peder could make out of one after such heavy digital modification.

"Okay, so if it's not drift EP, then phased crystal would do it."

"Nah, I've looked into that, too, and that won't work either."

Another huff. "Look, if you're just trying to break into your boss's superbase in Oslo, then fucking say so; don't give me this whole song and dance."

Peder smirked at himself—so much for 'delicate steering.' "Yep, you got me. That's what I'm looking for."

"All right, then you're going to need one Bunker Special, which is a ghost electron array—that's what you were looking for, right?"

"Uh-huh."

"How many transmitters and how many receivers do you need?"

"Three transmitters and two dozen receivers." In reality he only had sixteen commanders he needed to give receivers to, but saying 'sixteen' exactly would give away his plan. And just rounding it up to 'twenty' would still be too obvious. Saying 'two dozen' seemed like just the right amount of obfuscation.

"Okay," the voice continued, "now normally this would cost seventy-five k. But for wasting my time and insulting my intelligence let's call it a hundred thousand."

Peder sighed. "Eighty."

"Ninety."

"Eighty-five."

"Fine. So eighty-five it is—*if* you can wait six to eight weeks for delivery. If you want it this week ..."

Peder sighed again. "And I do ... "

"Then that's one twenty."

"One hundred."

"One twenty."

"One ten."

"This isn't the negotiation part; we did that already."

Peder issued a final sigh. "Fine, one twenty. I'll just need it before Friday," he asserted.

"Right. You'll get the details about the pickup."

Well, he had cost himself extra by trying to be cute, but otherwise he had come away with exactly what he needed.

Still, even after Peder had this ghost electron array, he still had no way of distributing the receivers to his men—nor even of seeing them at all. Which led him to the next calls on his agenda ...

Chapter 14 - Skeleton

As their truck turned a corner, Janus yelled, "—Stop!" He slammed on the manual brakes in case the truck's autodriver was slow responding to his verbal command.

"What?" asked Mohr.

Janus pointed to a deer carcass lying ahead in the road. "Fuck, Hartley!" he yelled at one of the men in the back. "You said this route was clear!"

"It *is!*" Hartley insisted. "Or I thought it was ... "

They all looked into their OHUDs, referring to the up-to-the-minute map that showed the location of every mine and autonomous weapons array in Oslo.

Except Mohr, who looked at Janus calmly and said, "Just drive."

"But that deer got wasted. There could be more mines on this road—"

"Janus, does that deer look like it was blown up by a mine to you?"

Looking again, they noted the deer was mostly intact with only its entrails spilling out into the road. This was the work of natural violence, not high explosives.

"Huh. Guess not," admitted Janus. He set the truck back on its route.

Their team was understandably jumpy, as they had wandered into an unmarked minefield just the day before. They had only realized it when they had spotted a deer carcass that had exploded like a venison piñata. They hit the brakes, called back to HQ to double-check, and found that a minelayer unit had booby-trapped the street that day. They had just forgotten to commit their additions to the friendly ordnance map so that other corporate army units could steer clear of it. The mines were deactivated remotely, and Mohr's men backed out. And by the next morning the minelayer's commander was missing a few teeth, courtesy of Janus and Hartley.

Their truck rumbled back on its way.

"So, Captain ... " said Hartley, "we doing more of this shit tomorrow?"

"Yup," replied Mohr.

"Fuck ... Haven't we done enough already? 'Cause it's getting like Russian Roulette just to take a drive around here ... "

"Yeah," interjected Styles. "I mean there's a bunch of idiots out there laying mines. They got us rigging anti-air sites. Other teams are planting ambushes and tripwires. A lot of other units are doing the exact same things. And for *three days* now? ... I mean, what are we building out here—North Korea or something?"

"Or something," said Mohr.

Honestly he had his own misgivings. But, when he had arrived in Oslo a few days ago and beheld the Bunker, he realized that he had long ago sold his soul to the Devil. And now that he was down in the

Inferno and living on Hell's insurance plan, it would be silly for him to cavil about the missions he was sent on.

A minute later they pulled up outside of a twenty-story residential, their destination. "Everybody out," said Janus. They circled around to the back of their truck and pulled off the last pallet. Three of them carried it into the building, and meanwhile Mohr brought along their portable generator.

Inside, Hartley wired the generator into the building's lift trunk. It made some flickering starts and stops before supplying steady power to the system. Mohr's men had more of this duty tomorrow, and he hoped their generator held out. Equipment in the Bunker was tight for some reason, and, if this generator failed, they would be hauling these pallets up the stairs themselves. —*Stairs*, Mohr iterated. What a medieval mode of elevation. They should just declare them 'de-invented' and find ways to deal with it.

The elevator delivered them to the thirteenth floor, where they stepped out into a tomb. Heavy dust and dirt lined the carpets, and they were traced with scant footprints. The walls were scraped with claw marks, showing how the building's starving pets had fought it out after the evacuation.

They followed their OHUD maps to apartment 1312. The front door had been broken into long ago like all the others. The map next pointed them to the bedroom. Hartley was the first to see inside, and he made an exclamation and recoiled.

Following him in, Mohr found a Human skeleton lying sideways on the bed, a knife embedded in its chest. With the body's tissues decomposed, the knife was resting between the ribs as in a macabre cutlery rack.

Mohr had seen many such scenes in his first year in Oslo. So many, in fact, that he felt he had been field-educated in the Sherlock Holmesian art of coaxing out the narrative of a crime. Here he noted how the knife was a plain kitchen implement and not a dedicated weapon—an instrument of extemporaneous rather than premeditated violence. The fact that it had been left behind also said that the killer had done his work and run.

He reasoned that the victim had been someone who had refused to evacuate, staying behind until the gangs had started stripping down apartment buildings. When some thugs at last burst through this door and found someone still inside, an already violent act took a simply more violent turn. Afterwards there had been no need to dispose of the body as this would have been months after the Singularity, with few left to care about any more dead bodies. He could also assume that the victim had been a woman by the plain and awful fact that the body had been found on a bed.

The four of them set the pallet they were carrying down in front of the windows. Pulling back the shades unfurled another floor-to-ceiling vantage on Oslo's outskirts, looking north and west.

In well-practiced routine, they began deploying the missile pallet. Mohr clicked through the machine's activation routines in his OHUD: one to boot and run its integrity tests; one to deploy its feet and stabilize itself; another to deploy its launching barrels and orient them facing out of the window; one more to make a tactical survey and fire-map its view.

Styles retrieved a small pack from the plat's side that contained nanoexplosive patches. He placed these on the window in a circle around the launch tubes' view. Since these windows were made of nanoglass, special explosives were needed to fragment them before the missiles were launched. Otherwise the missiles would either ricochet back into the bedroom, or tear the whole window out of its frame. Either outcome set the odds against the missiles hitting their target.

After the platform had passed a connection and readiness test, Mohr fed the system its final arming code. It contacted HQ, wired into the defense net, and needed only one more safety release before it was hot. Thereafter it would be dedicated to the routine of spotting flying objects out of the window, interrogating them with its IFF, and firing on any of which it disapproved.

"So, done for the day, right?" said Styles.

"Almost," said Mohr. He gestured to the skeleton.

Styles gave a questioning look, but the three others proceeded to the corners of the bed. Styles caught on and went to the fourth. Mohr leaned forward, picked the knife out of the chest, and threw it away. The rest of them pulled up the comforter and wrapped the remains inside. Janus and Styles carried it between them, keeping it as straight and undisturbed as possible. Styles wanted to make a remark about how light the body was, but something made him bite it back.

Mohr had also done his share of burials during his year in Oslo. When he had found his first few bodies, there were still EMTs and coroners left in the city, so he would send them the location and the body would be collected. But, once those services had pulled out, Mohr found all of his postings going untended. He had tried to shirk this off, but then he would hear other men back at base joking about the 'floaters' or 'dog foods' they had come across in the city. After that, at the end of every day, Mohr would bury one of the bodies in his backlog.

On this return to Oslo, he had been hoping this rule would no longer be necessary. This was his first discovery to the contrary.

Outside there was little open ground. They did brief scans with penetrating sensors until they found a stretch of sidewalk that had no dormant water mains or sewer lines beneath it. They shattered the concrete with their sonic hammer and removed the pieces. Then they went to spades and shovels and dug the grave the old-fashioned way. Fifteen minutes later they had finished interring the remains.

They stood over the nameless resting place.

"Does someone usually ... say something now?" asked Styles.

Mohr huffed at him slightly. The man did not understand that this was one of those simple acts of kindness due between Human beings. Despite all the ceremony attached to burial, in its primal form it was just a plain courtesy to be rendered in mute apostrophe.

But, to answer Styles's prompting, Mohr swung his spade over his shoulder and said to the grave:

"Rest in peace now."

They turned and walked back to their truck.

Chapter 15 - Grey Gold

Erlend was driving himself and Märtha on the expressway out of Vestvågøy. He was assigned to inspect the nanoconstruction fallout shelters Leknes was building, and Kitano had given Märtha one of her rare permissions to tag along. The Lontan Governate had supplied the construction kits only days ago, and the Home Guard was quickly installing them on every island in the archipelago.

They took a groundcar since that was the most fuel-efficient option for tackling the long stretches of the old European Route highways. The expressway shed its lanes one by one on the way out of the city. By the time they reached the first bridge to another island, it had shriveled to just a two-lane road.

Märtha had long known that Leknes was located in an archipelago, but this had always been a merely encyclopedic fact for her. In the city her vision was always crowded by augspace and her hearing deafened by the bustle of habitation. But, after crossing that first bridge, she found them striking out into dazzling and uncluttered terrain.

Beyond Vestvågøy, Lofoten's many islands were small, tree-covered peaks that rose at abrupt slants out of the water. It was like a mountain range that had been flooded to become a forest of summits. At sea level each island wore a narrow skirt of flat land, and Mankind had wedged its way onto all of these with its highways and hamlets. Driving those stretches, out one side of the car would be an island's great pile of stone, its presence tolling as an inaudibly deep bell. And out the other would be the endless ocean, the surf agitated only by the distant calls of the sea birds.

At length they arrived at the first nanoconstruction site. This one was merely a day old: a survey team had scouted the location and planted the nanite seeds only last evening. Overnight the nanites had suffused the ground, building a stretching resource lattice and preparing for the true work to come the next day. But this work was all subterranean, such that, when Märtha and Erlend arrived, the only above-ground signs of progress were a few patches of steaming grey gold, bubbling up like oil. There were no more than a dozen of these patches over the entire forty-meter 'kill floor'—so named because anything in that region that was not wearing a safety transponder was free to be atomically digested.

Astride the construction site there was a container full of metal bar stock. At the back of the container two men were pulling out three-meter metal bars and depositing them onto hoversleds. These bars were the timber of this new construction process, all uniform in size but color-coded to show their constituent elements. Once the men had loaded a hoversled with a dozen of these, another worker would shuttle the sled out onto the field and dump the contents into one of the pools of grey goo. The nanites would melt and consume the metals in seconds, but with seemingly little effect.

Märtha was filled with questions, so she figured she had better start asking.

"What are they doing?" she posed to Erlend in her first broad sally.

Erlend turned from the foreman he had been speaking to. "Supplying the nanites with raw materials," he replied, and turned back.

"But why do they need raw materials?" Märtha persisted. "I thought nanotech just ... made whatever it needed out of what was in the ground."

The foreman gave Erlend an expressionless look. Erlend turned back to Märtha:

"Ah. You're thinking of *alchemy*. That's a closely related field to nanotechnology, but somewhat different. With these shake-and-bake kits the Lontans gave us, the most they can do is work with the elements that are already in the ground. They can't use fusion to make different ones. So they still need supplements of aluminium, tungsten, and whatever else they don't find down there."

"But isn't carbon all you need?"

Erlend was becoming a little hassled now. "*If* we were just making a solid-diamond tomb fit for a pharaoh, then yes, carbon's all you need. But a fallout shelter needs air conditioning, ductwork, refrigeration ... Not all things that can be made out of diamond."

"And then why don't we see anything built yet?"

113

"Well, there's a lot that's been built, but it's all underground. When the fallout shelter's done, it'll be twenty stories below ground and only some entrances up here."

Sensing it was time to desist, Märtha turned back to watch the field.

She found the construction progress disappointingly slow. By her expectations, this 'kill floor' should have long ago become a volcanic morass of nanoactivity. Yet the pools of active grey goo were sparse and quiet, no matter how much bar stock the workers dumped into them. Compared to the other examples of nanotech Märtha had seen in action, this moved at a geriatric pace.

... But then she realized that she had never actually seen nanotech in action—just anti-nanotech propaganda vids. Simulated grey goo and ecological disasters; time-lapse clips from the Singularity. But the plain, un-sensationalized technology itself was underwhelming.

The one thing that had impressed her, though, was the heat. The grey gold may have appeared inert, but it was still radiating raw Kelvins as potently as a lava flow. The workers running metal stock out into the field were so slick with sweat that they were wearing only work boots and swimming trunks. A table of water cups was set up for them back at the trailer, and they downed shots like endurance runners with every lap back. Märtha wanted to ask Erlend why the men did not have any special gear, but she could imagine the obvious answer was cost. They could either equip all of the men with volcanologist-grade heat suits, or just have them stripped down and passing fluids like Death Valley marathoners.

The sight of those workers, however, struck her as counterintuitive. She had always heard of nanotech as some insidious invention threatening to tear loose from Human reigns. But how dangerous and advanced could it be if it still required an unskilled labor force to sweat like pyramid slaves? —And ones wearing swimming trunks, even?

They went on to visit a dozen other construction sites that day. Seeing those farthest along, Märtha began to be impressed by the true speed of nanotechnology. While its progress was invisible to the naked eye, it was still erecting structures in days that would have taken last-century Humans months or years of toil. But it did not eliminate all of the elbow grease, which still had to be supplied by some sweaty, sunburned roustabouts.

Returning to the base that night, Erlend and Märtha first checked in with Kitano—she insisted on seeing Märtha immediately after she returned, to verify that she had not been maimed while in Erlend's care. Märtha was then dispatched to her quarters for sleep.

After she was gone, Kitano said to Erlend, "We should get Märtha out of here."

Erlend looked after the girl's retreat. "She just left ... " he said, bewildered.

"No, I mean out of the Home Guard."

115

"Oh ... " ">Haven't you been saying that ever since we brought her on board?" he switched to secure texting. Not that he expected Märtha to be eavesdropping out in the corridor, but no reason not to be careful.

">Yes, but there's something big coming up now—it's obvious. / That crazy drill at the beginning of the week. / Now this rush to build fallout shelters ... "

Erlend grumbled. ">You have a point." And he was aware of even more troubling facts than those.

">God forbid something does happen with this emergency, she'll want to be involved. / And we may all be so busy that she'll slip through a crack somewhere and get hurt. / She'll be safer out of the Home Guard."

">All right," Erlend conceded. ">School will be starting up soon. / How about we dump her into the Leknes system?"

">How about getting her out of here tomorrow?"

">Err, a little abrupt, don't you think? / She might think we were firing her. / Or she'd just be hurt—fragile teenage emotions and all that. / Let's give her a bit to prepare. / We should be okay through the weekend, anyway."

">Okay. / I'll tell Hanssen."

Chapter 16 - The Embassy

Willoch had been summoned by the Lontan Ambassador. His request had been impeccably worded and flawlessly polite—as always—, but it was still a summons. Asking would she 'please appear immediately' for an 'urgent discussion.' The regular Willoch would have done her duty and tripped over herself complying. But this new Willoch felt differently. Maybe it was her exhausted patience or her severe sleep deprivation, but she was considering confronting him. She wanted to barge into his office shouting 'Enough bullshit!' and accuse him of collaborating with the Hezokeen.

She was firmly convinced that he was behind their siege. He had certainly sold out their planet's location to the pirates, and, whatever his complicity since, he had done precious little to alleviate the situation. And her frustration was exacerbated by the knowledge of what the Lontans would do in case the Hezokeen did attack: pursuant to their lofty policy of *laissez-faireism*, they would simply evacuate to their Embassy and depart the battle zone. Human independence had to be respected, even to the point of letting them fight—and perish—alone.

When she entered the Ambassador's office, she had just mustered the audacity to do this—and she might have had she found him sitting idly in his chaise longue as always. But instead he was standing back near his office windows where there was a man-sized portal carved out of the glass and leading down a tunnel into space. Willoch stopped and stared.

"Ah, thank you for seeing me, Admiral," the Ambassador said first. "Especially during this desperately busy week."

"Ambassador ... " she said, mystified. "Of course we always have time to spare for our benefactors." She had wanted this to sound sarcastic, but because of her surprise she forgot to salt it properly. It came out sounding blandly polite.

"I will come to the point," the Ambassador continued. "The Governor has decided that it is time we informed you fully of your situation with the pirate fleet."

"... Informed *me*?"

"No, we will release the same details to all of the Eyes governments shortly. But we would like to give the facts to a Human officer face-to-face. And by doing so we wish to correct the misunderstandings that have arisen between us. I know, for instance, that you consider me to be in league with the Hezokeen. That you believe it was I who divulged the location of your planet to them. Though I do not take offense at this. It is merely the result of the Zaichi Ambassador's interference, and my own necessary silence."

Willoch was beyond dumbstruck. The conspiracy she had sought to uncover had that quickly unmasked itself?

"We wish to re-convince you—and through yourself your leaders—of Lontan intentions," the Ambassador added.

Willoch was wavering between two emotions. First was incredulity at this whole turn—the Ambassador was calling out her suspicions just as she had meant to bring them to a head, which could only mean that he was blowing smoke. But second was a child-like shame at ever having doubted. The Lontans were so advanced that, if they were actually 'evil'—really, truly *evil*—, then why had they let Willoch harbor any suspicions at all? They could reach into her brain and expurgate anything not to their liking. But instead they had given her the freedom to doubt, and that implied that they really had nothing to hide.

And Willoch felt a powerful wish to succumb to this second emotion. The last month had seen a fatal crash in all her stocks of confidence. She had begun by doubting the Lontans, then next the Zaichi, and in the end she had trusted no one. Yet Humanity was doomed in the face of such a conniving universe. She needed an ally, even if it meant having to swallow her pride, admit she had been misled, and run back to a lapsed allegiance.

"Very well," she said simply. "Is that ... " She motioned at the portal beside the Ambassador, but found no more intelligent words to continue her question with.

"A shuttle to convey us to the Embassy," the Ambassador explained. "For a meeting with the Governor."

Willoch nearly went wide-eyed. No Human had ever been inside the Embassy. That was why the Lontans surrounded it with an information shield impenetrable to all sensors.

"Come," the Ambassador said, and he gestured down the tunnel.

Willoch proceeded cautiously inside. At the end of the tunnel she exited onto the 'shuttle,' which was nothing more than a naked platform parked in the space outside of the Ambassador's office. She gasped as she turned around, beholding the bustling exterior of Gateway Station. Its reaching architecture filled an entire hemisphere of her vision, and there seemed to be nothing insulating them from the vacuum.

Turning away from the station she saw the awful blackness of space. She knew in principle that this void stretched on for countless light-years, but, with no detail in the scene, she could imagine the blackness pressing in on her. Infinite suddenly became claustrophobic.

The Ambassador emerged onto the platform after her, and the portal linking the 'shuttle' to the station vanished.

"—Oh, excuse me," he said, and suddenly the black vista became sprinkled with stars. He had sensed her unease, and so had painted a holographic veneer over the emptiness.

"Thank you," Willoch mumbled, a little embarrassed by her reaction.

Two chairs melded out of the floor, one some Swedish jungle gym contraption that the Ambassador took—an authentic Lontan chair—, and the other a shallow bowl, which Willoch reasoned was for her.

Gateway fell away as the shuttle shot off at a fantastic rate. Willoch grabbed her seat for stability—before realizing that there had not been the slightest lurch of acceleration. She whiplashed around to see the station shrinking vanishingly fast behind them. She also caught sight of the Earth in the backdrop. While the station winked into nothingness in seconds, the Earth contracted only slightly. She took this as an illustration of scale: Gateway Station – tiny and insignificant; the planet Earth – slightly less so.

Willoch tried to contain her overwhelmedness, but the Ambassador's 'shock and awe' approach was working. This was merely the cab ride over to the Embassy and already she was mesmerized. To inoculate herself against further surprise, she knew she had to drop her expectations of mere technology and brace for unabashed magic. She tried to adopt the attitude that the Lontans were omniscient and omnipotent and omnipuissant—by way of shorthand she bundled all those up and simply called them 'omniomnical.'

"So, Ambassador ... " she said, trying to use conversation to stay composed, "you said we were going to meet the Governor. But ... why on the Embassy? Doesn't he have an office on Gateway?" She was only curious, but she realized too late that this might sound ungrateful.

"He does," the Ambassador replied, "but we hope that taking you to the Embassy will be a small divulgence on our part. One that will help rebuild the trust between our peoples."

Willoch nodded. "Inside will I see what Lontan culture is really like?" She was imagining the Embassy as a much more modern and cosmopolitan version of Gateway, with aliens of all shapes and sizes strolling promenades, browsing at shops, commuting to work ... Though she quickly realized how naive that vision was. The Embassy was likely nothing more than a computer simulation busied with alien consciousnesses.

"Oh, no, not on such a remote outpost as this," the Ambassador replied.

"Then where would I have to go? What *is* Lontan culture really like?"

"I could tell you, if you would let me erase your memory afterwards."

Willoch laughed, considering it a joke. But the Ambassador's demeanor told her otherwise. "You're serious?" She did not need to consider the bargain at all: "Okay, shoot."

"Lontan civilization is like anything you can imagine."

Willoch was crestfallen, souring at the non-answer. "No, I mean honestly."

122

"I am being truthful. Lontan civilization is so widespread that it has variegated to an effectively infinite degree."

Belatedly Willoch realized that he was telling the truth. "Ah, I should have imagined—you have colonized three galaxies after all ... Though that 'erase your memory' ploy was a little much."

But the Ambassador 'grinned.' "Oh, we have colonized many more than three galaxies."

Willoch paused ... But then she deciphered this, too: "Oh yes, there are ... three dozen galaxies in the Local Group, I believe? So only the three *major* ones: the Milky Way, Andromeda, and Triangulum; but—"

"Oh, *magnitudes* more than that."

Willoch now stopped. There was no more flinching from those implications. "The Lontans have spread *outside* of the Local Group of galaxies?"

"Actually we *started* outside of the Local Group. When we arrived here two hundred thousand years ago it was from the neighboring supercluster. But we told the Milky Way species that we had come from Triangulum; we told the Triangulum species that we had come from Andromeda; and we told the Andromeda species that we had come from here."

Willoch's jaw dropped. It was such an astounding lie—and to what purpose? She felt the world spinning out of control ... Yet she was

123

voracious for the details the Ambassador was suddenly meting out.

"But why the deception? Why not simply say where you'd really come from?"

"It would have been too intimidating to the younger species."

Willoch stared. "Where *did* you really come from?"

"Our native star lies far outside of your observable universe—on the order of a Teraparsec distant. You do not even have a name for the galaxy it is in."

Willoch was amazed—a trillion light-years away ... So the Lontans saying that they had come from the neighboring galaxy was a lie of a millionfold understatement.

"But that's impossible!" she objected. "Your species may have been spacefaring for a million years, but, even with the fastest hyperdrives, you couldn't have traversed that distance! ... —Well, unless you were also lying about how old you were."

"Of course," he nodded.

Willoch frowned. "But, still ... the time scales are so tremendous! And there's so much empty space out there! How could you cross the supervoids between the galaxy filaments? You'd have to travel for centuries without there being even an atom of hydrogen to re-supply with."

"I'll let you in on another secret. Crossing those distances is impractical with your current hyperdrives, yes. They are machines that contract distances by fantastic exponents: fifteen magnitudes, twenty. But, if you can only contract space to some finite degree, then all you have done is reduced travel times, not eliminated them. The hyperdrive has knit the stars together, but what about the galaxies? The superclusters? The filaments? Eventually the universe will present you with a distance that you cannot cross."

Willoch thought she had deciphered his clues. "Ahh, of course ... You developed some propulsion *beyond* the hyperdrive," she said, intrigued.

"Actually we only carried the hyperdrive to its peak. For your current drives, transiting up each band takes exponentially more energy. That is why, with the reactors we provide you, you can only reach up to $I_b$band—twenty-four transitions. This limits you to interstellar travel. But long ago we found a different way to tackle that energy barrier. It still takes an absurd amount of energy, but with it we can transit practically without limit: up a thousand bands, ten thousand, a *million*. Think of what is possible *then*."

Willoch glimpsed this ... and she was awed. She had been trained to visualize hyperspace contraction as a sphere whose radius shrank geometrically with every transition up to a new band. Their existing drives could shrink that sphere microscopically, but what the Ambassador was describing was shrinking it to a dimensionless point—until the entire universe was written on a grain of sand. Once in that infinitely high band of hyperspace, it would take only a little finessing of one's 'exit dither' while transiting back out to reappear at any other place in the universe. Traveling without moving.

So the hyperdrives on their ships were not magnificently advanced tools for contracting space. They were actually very primitive and restricted foldspace engines. The Lontans were giving Humans and the other Milky Way species access only to the entry levels of hyperspace, letting them incrementally cheat the light-speed limit. But at its zenith hyperspace meant the total abolition of scale.

"Ever since we discovered foldspace technology," the Ambassador continued, "we've been exploring and colonizing on a truly universal scale. Whenever we encounter other sentient species, however, we concoct a redacted history so as not to alarm them. Many species will accept neighbors from another star or galaxy, but they pale to think that someone has already beaten them to 'everywhere.' Which is what we did here—posing as your big brothers from Triangulum."

"Okay, I see the sense in that," Willoch admitted. "But have you colonized *everything?*" she asked with concern.

"Oh, goodness, no. Not nearly."

Willoch was relieved.

"For all of the universe that we've explored, it would take us trillions of years to fill it up. Yet we can tentatively say that we are the first species to spread so far."

"Really?"

"We have discovered countless other spacefaring species, of course. Some even possessing or pursuing hypertechnology. But none have achieved our success or scale of expansion."

"What are the odds of that? That across the entire universe there's no one more advanced?"

"Well, what you should be asking is, given that there *is* such a species that is so advanced, what are the odds that you would *not* be talking to them right now?"

Willoch nodded admittingly.

"But even *a priori* the odds are not terribly remote, as it turns out. The universe is thirteen billion years old, yes, but it started out as only a sea of hydrogen. The next eight billion years were spent merely watching countless stars undergo successive fusion deaths to seed the universe with heavier elements—the carbon, nitrogen, and oxygen that our species were built from. All of us were born under the first generation of stars with planets complex enough to support higher forms of life.

"And we can actually calculate from raw observation how long it should take a species to develop foldspace technology. When you consider all of the probabilistic factors—the rarity of sentient life, of technological progress, of interstellar prosperity, of foldspace discovery, and of even *wanting* to explore the universe—, then the

127

expected number of Lontan-like species we should be seeing by now is 0.92. So we are actually just a little ahead of the curve."

As he spoke, Willoch was looking around at the stars and envisioning every point planted with a Lontan flag. She fancied that even the shapes of the constellations could be the Lontans' work: the result of a hundred thousand years of galaxy-scale flower arrangement. —Of course the Lontans would not have arranged the constellations for Earth's benefit, but it was the very idea that there might rightly be a trademark symbol hanging off of Orion or the Big Dipper ... In her formation of 'omniomnical,' she now had to include a literal 'omnipresent.'

"But why give us Milky Way species the hyperdrive and not foldspace?" she asked. "Why restrict us to just interstellar travel?"

"Why not?" the Ambassador replied easily. "What need have you to explore the edges of the universe versus the uncharted regions of your own galaxy? Your Milky Way is barely settled, so why direct your energies elsewhere?"

Willoch could not argue with that.

"Though, once you had filled up this galaxy, we would have considered giving you greater mobility. —If you were ready for it."

"'If we were ready'?" Willoch repeated accusingly.

"That must sound like simple elitism to you, but please think of it as 'empirical elitism.' We Lontans have observed so many species that we can easily tell the children and adolescents from the adults. Certain technologies bring certain responsibilities, and you are simply not ready for the next levels."

This piqued Willoch ... but she forced herself to accept it. The Ambassador was right that such amassed experience as theirs was its own force of argument. Willoch gainsaying him would be like a three-year-old criticizing a retirement plan.

After reflection, she realized the answer to her original question: "So that's what Lontan culture is like. Spread everywhere across the universe, playing God with the lesser species. ... A benevolent tyranny?"

"Granted," the Ambassador cocked his head. "But the chief ramification of foldspace technology is that the universe is simply too small. The light speed barrier would have ensured the impracticality of empires even a hundred star systems in size. It would have put an irreducible lag on conquest and ambition. But, with foldspace, it is possible for one being—one will—to assert itself everywhere. Discovering this, we Lontans realized that, in the limit, the universe would gravitate towards one form of tyranny or another. We believe it has been our great service to at least give it the prefix of 'benevolent.'"

Willoch found herself automatically forming objections and arguments, but again she quieted them. While this unipolarity was inherently sinister, she had to admit that, if the Lontans had truly wished to be tyrannical, then they would not even be having this conversation. Fifty years ago the Earth would have ended up as a fly crushed on the grill of one of the Lontans' world reactors, sent to digest all of the Sol system down into its constituent elements. But instead the Lontans had declared the Earth a protected planet and were cultivating its indigenous, tool-using apes into an interstellar power. To call this mere 'benevolence' was an egregious act of gift-horsing—'omnibenevolent' she now had to add to her characterization.

But, she realized, there was no guarantee that Lontan behavior here was indicative of their behavior everywhere. That they were 'experimenting' with the Milky Way implied that the Lontans were running a battery of tests across countless other galaxies. Even if they had no sinister intentions, there would have to be suffering. A doctor testing a new medicine had to have control groups that were fed only placebos, and some patients had to be given outrageous or feckless variations on the treatment. With the Lontans testing their own 'regimen' on a palette as wide as the universe, there had to be whole superclusters that were being likewise shortchanged.

"Ah, but now we are arriving at the Embassy," the Ambassador interjected, "and I'm afraid I must wipe your memory of this conversation."

"What? ... —Oh, that was what you meant before? But wait, I just have a few more—"

130

The Ambassador rose and said, "We have arrived."

Willoch was surprised that the flight had gone so quickly. But then that was the Lontans, she admitted.

131

Chapter 17 - The Governor

Willoch saw nothing outside of the shuttle. She was about to ask the Ambassador if the Embassy was invisible—when she glanced up and saw a gigantic, black-mirrored sphere ahead. Its diameter must have been tens of kilometers, and she could only slightly perceive the perspective parallax that said they were hurtling towards it.

They were swallowed by a featureless tunnel and flew into the structure. After a minute they slowed and the tunnel opened up into a large, spherical space. It was bisected by a transparent floor, and the shuttle was rising towards a hole in it that was sculpted to admit its outline. It threaded through and stopped when its surface became flush, then melded seamlessly into it.

She looked to the Ambassador for instructions, and he gestured her forward. After a few steps, she turned to see if he was following, but he had noiselessly disappeared. Turning back she was startled to see a new-appeared Human standing before her: the well-known image of the Lontan Governor's customary mannequin.

"Pleased to meet you in person at last, Admiral Willoch," he said in English.

"—Governor, sir," Willoch replied, approaching. She extended her hand—then thought too late that he must be a matterless hologram, which made this a gaffe on her part.

Yet he surprisingly caught her hand in a firm shake. More Lontan technological prowess.

"Pardon me for donning Human form," the Governor said, "and for speaking in English. If it were just the two of us, then I would of course use Norwegian; but a record of this meeting will be sent to all of the Eyes. And, with how imprecise translation is, only the original spoken words can be taken to be official, and Russia and China are far more adept at handling English transcripts than Norwegian ones."

"No, this is perfectly fine," said Willoch, replying in English.

The Governor motioned off to the side at two Human chairs, which they took seats in.

"The purpose of this audience," he began easily, "is to inform you and the Human governments fully about your situation with the Hezokeen. I lament that the details have been kept from you thus far, but I hope you shall accept our reasons for doing so as I reveal them. Do you have any questions before we start?"

"... Yes, sir. I would like to know right away why you kept the truth from us," said Willoch, recovering some boldness.

The Governor nodded. "When the Hezokeen first arrived, we could deduce the truth behind their appearance very quickly. But there was little we ourselves could do about it, so why inform you? Humanity is under constant surveillance by our—and thus your—enemies, and you simply do not

133

have the technological means to keep a secret from them. So for us to give you any information is tantamount to giving it to them. This is why we only share certain things with you once they become critical for you to know. And that is precisely what we are doing now."

"But it's our planet and our system. Don't we have a right to know?"

"No."

"No?" Willoch was incredulous.

"Rights are not something you simply arrogate by saying, 'I have a right to X.' The current scope of accepted rights is determined by society—by an extrinsic consensus. So you have asked whether you have a 'right to know whatever we Lontans know concerning you.' Since we Lontans occupy at least an equal part in this extrinsic consensus, we must say that you do not."

Willoch bristled at this heavy-handed rebuttal, but that was the Governor's typical behavior. One might have expected the arbiter of Humanity's first contact to be a honey-voiced diplomat, but in reality he was simply brusque. He asserted Lontan policy, and he explained it up to a point, but that was it.

"But I can assure you," the Governor added, "that we have always acted in Humanity's best interests. Whatever we have kept from you was not out of stinginess or greed, but from an earnest desire to protect your people. Can you accept this?"

Willoch was only slightly mollified, but replied positively.

134

"Good. So, to begin, have you ever heard of a species called the Eththelnt?"

"It sounds familiar, actually ... " By reflex Willoch tried to look up the name in her OHUD encyclopedia, but having no net access became a stumbling block.

"They were the only other species that offered a serious bid to host your first contact. They came in second—behind us, of course. They are a moderately powerful species whose territory spreads diffusely across two thousand light-years. In this section of the galaxy they are actually near-rivals for us."

"Rivals?" Willoch could not muffle her concern. She was as a child finding out her parents could no longer protect her.

"Well, we Lontans are running a galaxy-scale civilization, and some parts of it are underpowered versus others. Observe:"

He motioned off to the side, where a holo of the Milky Way—or 'Gamma Galaxy,' as it was known in the Lontan system—had appeared. It was colored as a political map, Balkanized by countless three-dimensionally intertwining pseudopods, one for every species and faction. The Lontans held by far the largest demesne: a pink-colored mass, centered on the Galactic Core, reaching octopodally out into every crevice of the Milky Way. All its regions were shaded a different intensity, and, while the Core was a saturated pink, the arms faded away to ghostly translucency—evidently a coarse

135

approximation to the region's population and energy density.

The map zoomed in on an outer region of the galaxy where the local Lontan territory was colored so thin a shade as to suggest a vacant hinterland. Opposing it was a red-shaded region—for the Eththelnt—of similar size and slightly greater 'density' than the local Lontan arm it faced. This allayed Willoch's fears, as the Eththelnt were only 'rivals' because they were not facing off against the Lontan A Team—nor even their Y or Z Team.

"Ours and the Eththelnt's frontier territories are still well separated," continued the Governor, "so there is a large tract of free space in between us." The map highlighted the region between the nearest arms of these empires, perhaps fifty star systems wide. Taken in the context of the entire Lontan realm, it was no more than a synaptic gap at the end of a 40,000–light-year axon. "It is over this region that we and the Eththelnt have been fighting for around a millennium."

"A thousand years? Over that?" Willoch balked. "But by now the casualties on both sides must be unimaginable."

"Oh, please do not think us barbarians. It is a 'gentleman's war' as you might call it. Sentient beings are rarely ever slain, and, if they are, it is only because they bring it on themselves. Galactic warfare has evolved to the point where only a handful of consciousnesses are needed to control even vast military forces. When there are battles, it is all unmanned, unintelligent machines that do the fighting. —And the 'dying,' as it were," he added with hesitation. "We are only pitting resources, technologies, and industrial bases against each other. It is like any abstract game—chess, say. Pieces are lost and exchanged, but the two combatants never stoop to doing each other actual physical harm."

Willoch was first eased by this explanation, but that quickly faltered. When war could be waged at no Human cost—no cost in *life*, she corrected—then when did it end? Earth's wars may be horrible, but at least they were over in a few years, not a few thousand. ... —Well, no *single* Human war ever took a thousand years, but had they not been fighting individual ones back-to-back for far longer?

"But I don't understand," she protested. "It's such a small region of space. Surely it can't mean that much to you. Couldn't you and the Eththelnt simply expand elsewhere?"

"It may seem small, but that buffer zone still contains thousands of stars and planets. Whoever controls it, whoever colonizes and develops it, will tap energy and resources worth empires in the long run. And we Lontans think of nothing but the long run.

"Look ahead to when Gamma Galaxy fills up and the stars run out. That is still hundreds of thousands of years away at current colonization rates, but, by then, whether or not we have 'played for keeps' during the million-year land grab beforehand will make a great difference in how much territory we end up with.

"This war is also part of a meta-strategy with the Eththelnt to tie up each other's local resources. While we are both busy fighting over this region, neither of us can expand as freely or as quickly into the neighboring ones. And a slow, open war draws on us steadily, keeping us from falling into a cold war or stockpiling ruinous amounts of weaponry."

"I suppose ... " Willoch answered. Staring at the map, she ventured, "Still, your territory is so much larger than the Eththelnt's. Why don't you simply pool a few ships from your other regions and ... *win?*"

"Our territory may be large, yes, but it is also *large*. Pooling forces from all over the domain into this one speck would be wasteful. Plus this is hardly our only contentious front, and we do not have the resources to supply them all from the Core. Instead, we require all of our systems and regions to be self-sufficient. Otherwise you can imagine that the bureaucratic draw to run all this would be beyond stupendous."

"But, even so, aren't you the most technologically advanced species? You basically gave us all the technologies we have, so you must have much more advanced ones that you could deploy in a war."

"That is true, but we hold our advanced technologies in strict reserve. By limiting ourselves

138

to fighting on even footing with our opponents, we are forced to be innovative and adaptive. This ensures that we continue to develop in unique and useful ways."

Willoch found that strangely magnanimous. The Lontans were fighting with one hand tied behind their back just for the challenge and experience of it.

"But, to return to our original discussion," said the Governor, "our war with the Eththelnt has been raging for many centuries. And hostilities have been at a maximum starting fifty years ago."

"Fifty years ... " said Willoch. "That coincides with our First Contact."

"Exactly. Indeed it was because we discovered your planet that hostilities increased. Our forces were just closing out a decades-long skirmish when one of our probes happened on the Sol System. You lie off to the side of this undeveloped region, but still in a commanding position. Both the Eththelnt and us would give an entire field navy to have a base established here.

"After your discovery, the fighting naturally had to cease in your region. A first contact mission had to be organized, and your space had to be protected—a twenty light-year quarantine established, and such. But this was just for show. In reality, your planet had automatically become the new battlefield between us."

"What difference could we make?"

"None at the moment. But a first contact species is the fastest-expanding force in the universe. When a species is shown how far behind the modern era it sits, it becomes so ready to absorb new technologies, to expand, and to carve its survival out of the heavens. And whoever supplies that expansion will receive an incredible economic boon. Inside of your protected zone, you could build a hundred-star domain in a handful of centuries, and all completely untouchable by the Eththelnt. Then, when you finally emerged from it, you would be a natural Lontan ally. Such an outcome, while centuries away, is still direful to them. They must do whatever they can to prevent it.

"Thus began a new battle in our war: one centered around Humanity. And the first action in it was to see who would manage your first contact, as that species would have the most direct influence on you. In that opening maneuver, we won—obviously, as otherwise you would be speaking to an Eththelnt governor right now. This was a setback for the Eththelnt, but, as I said, it was only the opening action. And, if anything, it only gave them the initiative, as they now have to win over the stewardship of your first contact. They have to replace us."

"How could they do that?"

"One way would be if we Lontans were shown guilty of grievous mismanagement. Then the First Contact Commission would force us to surrender our position to the Eththelnt, seeing as they were second-in-line at the time of bidding."

"That seems unlikely. Surely there's no species more experienced at managing first contacts than the Lontans."

"True. But we could be ejected if the request came from Humanity itself. And you might make such a request if your system were to suffer some catastrophe while under our care."

Willoch made the connection: "Some catastrophe ... via the Hezokeen."

The Governor nodded.

"So the *Eththelnt* hired them to blockade our system?"

"Yes."

"Which means *they* divulged the location of our planet."

"Precisely. We and the Eththelnt were the only two species privy to such knowledge, and they the only ones with a motive to reveal it."

"But ... then why was it the Zaichi Ambassador who tried to mislead me into thinking it was you?"

"It would have been too obvious for the Eththelnt Ambassador to do so himself. It is no secret that we and they are in conflict—it is right there in the War Matrix. It would have been obvious that they were only trying to discredit us, and their accusation would have cast suspicion on themselves.

"But the Eththelnt prefer to keep a low profile. Consider how you yourself had only dimly heard of them at the start of this conversation. Until they have a real chance to seize the stewardship of your system, they will remain in the shadows.

"As to why the Zaichi Ambassador, in particular, approached you, the Zaichi and the Eththelnt simply consider themselves co-belligerents versus us. Not surprising since nearly every pair of species will ally against us at one time or another."

Willoch was listening with an exterior calm that belied her true state of turmoil. She had always taken comfort in the idea that the Earth was too inconsequential to be in any danger. She had pictured Humanity as a student, being instructed by the Lontans, in an otherwise empty classroom, with no peers to outshine them or bullies to torment them. But this was an entirely different picture the Governor was painting.

"So the Hezokeen's true mission ... " she started, but broke off.

"Must be to raze your system and deal great damage to the Earth," the Governor answered plainly. "We do not know their exact target package or planned damage profile, of course, but that is most likely their objective."

Willoch was shocked to hear the demolition of her home planet posited so callously. "So the Hezokeen attack us, destroy everything ... and then whoever's left evicts the Lontans and welcomes in the Eththelnt?" she huffed in disbelief.

"The Eththelnt have been preparing for this for a long time. They have been infiltrating your society with mannequins and front companies for decades, which they will use to give them a powerful voice in public opinion after such a catastrophe. They have also been focusing their efforts on Mars and Venus. First, because those are the easiest planets to infiltrate; and second, because they could easily be left untouched if the Hezokeen have instructions only to attack the Earth."

Willoch recoiled. "But ... even if their plan works and the Eththelnt are brought in, won't it be that much harder for them to manage our first contact? To steward a wrecked world?"

"On the contrary, it would be far easier. In our first contacts, we Lontans take great care to raise a civilization to technological maturity while still maintaining its identity—this is a key tenet for us. That is why, for all of the technologies we have given you, your way of life is still much the same as it was before we came. Your customs and cultures have grown but held their roots.

"However, if the Eththelnt were brought in to rebuild after a Hezokeen attack, they would be facing a blank slate. With your species having had a brush with extinction, you would allow a flooding inrush of technology. Your knowledge would jump by millennia overnight. The Eththelnt would rebuild cities in days, reshape continents and oceans, build resource towers and wanderer factories. To make up the raw population gap they would bring in birthing vats and nöo-parenting. Your progress would be miraculous, phoenix-like.

"But then, ten or twenty years down the road, you would not be the same people. Perhaps still the same species with the same genetic blueprint, but neither born the same, nor living the same, nor with the same cultural memories.

"We Lontans have given you technology at such a pace that you are able to adapt it into who you are instead of vice versa. But, under the Eththelnt, while your species might survive, its identity would not."

Willoch appreciated these words, but they still made her prickle with irony. The Lontans may claim to be led by these lofty ideals, but they still had no qualms about using Humanity as a poker chip in their endless, high-stakes game of Empire.

Yet they were the only ones who could save them, so Willoch appealed to the Governor in desperation:

"Then you must do something to stop them! Now that they've brought in an outside force—now that they're interfering with our development, can't you ... send some of your own ships to reinforce us? Just enough to put us in parity with the Hezokeen so that they stand down? Maybe it would be enough for you just to show the flag?"

"I am sorry, but no. Open hostilities between us and the Eththelnt may have surceased in your immediate region, but they have escalated everywhere else. We are both fully engaged with little resources to spare."

"But can't you do *anything?*"

"We've already done it!" the Governor exclaimed. "Look at yourself: an Admiral in a fleet of over a hundred modern, Lontan-made warships. We sold you the vessels, the weapons, the infrastructure. We trained you, prepared you. But our help must stop somewhere. You must learn to stand on your own."

"How is this standing on our own? With all the ships and technologies you've sold us, we might as well be puppets—"

"No. We have given you the tools to fight the battle, but in the end Humans will make all the decisions, do all the fighting and the dying. *That* is standing on your own."

Willoch was struck, and she faltered into silence. The Governor had made his point.

Yet this still all seemed to her a coy way for the Lontans to absolve themselves of responsibility. To paint a convenient line in the sand past which they could wash their hands and proclaim, 'Not our problem.'

"You knew it would come to this all along," she said bitterly, looking into the Governor's eyes. "Some showdown where our species' survival was at stake. Our entire first contact was a game to you. A little diversion in your grand 'gentleman's war' where not a single Lontan or Eththelnt life is lost, but, if a billion Humans are killed, it's just 'knight takes pawn' to you, isn't it?"

The Governor met her stare unwaveringly. "What? Did you think it would be easy?"

Willoch almost gasped.

"That we Lontans would show up, build you into a modern utopia, and set you atop the stars with no risk at all? You might have known something was odd by the way we were treating you: being so expedient with technology, so urgent about building your defenses, supplying you with a military. If your species were not in a dangerous position, no one would have bothered with you.

"You remember when I said that we and the Eththelnt were the only two serious bids for your first contact? Do you know who the others were?"

Willoch shook her head.

"There were a dozen, and they were all wildly theocratic civilizations. The results of failed first contacts—of too much primitivism lasting into the stellar age. They file petitions to steward every newly discovered species simply because their faiths command them to go after new potential crops of believers. If they had won your contract, the only aliens ever to land here would have been missionaries, and they would have used technology as a lure, giving it to those who accepted their faith, and encouraging it be used against the unconverted. An effective way to enslave a planet."

Willoch stared downwards, trying to hold to her stubborn look.

146

"Now you are thinking," the Governor said, "that we Lontans should have left you alone. You think that at least you would have been safer that way. That, since your species had survived this long with so many threats hanging over it, that it would have endured."

Willoch looked up, her thoughts having been called out.

"But let me disaffect you of that. You have only the faith in your invincibility as of an untested soldier. But I am a first contact governor. I have studied the maturation of civilizations and know the raw probabilities by which they destroy themselves.

"It may surprise you, but there was actually a long period where we halted all first contacts and let species develop by themselves—to see if we were doing any good. And we ended up watching as most of them suffered global calamities, and fought wars that shed cities like single casualties.

"There are so many foolish reasons why. A civilization moving to the stars is at the most volatile period in its history. Beforehand their universe was limited to a single planet, but now they are about to embark into realms undreamed-of by their ancestors, to multiply and evolve without limit. It is a singular leaping-off where, in a myriad ways, the forces of new and old go to war. And you had so much of that brewing on your own world. Then enable all of that hostility with exponentially advancing technology, and ... " he gestured in extrapolation.

"But first contact always helps steer a species away from this course," he countered. "Not because you experience some grand 'coming-together,' but because it calls you to exchange all of your old *intra*-species prejudices for new *inter*-species ones. Because, for however different you are from each other, it is nothing compared to how different you are from us. It takes that shared distrust to pull you back from disaster.

"You may despise us for bringing this upon you, but it was the only way. And you are better off," he added as a verdict.

Willoch stayed downcast, avoiding the Governor's eyes. Her knee-jerk reaction was denial—to look at this person dispensing summary judgments and to think, 'Who the hell is he?' But that was the problem—he was a Lontan. And a first contact governor. No matter how much Willoch disliked what he said, she knew it had to be the truth.

"Is there ... any chance that the Eththelnt are not behind this?" she asked. "That these Hezokeen aren't just some over-aggressive pirates?"

"No. That was one of the reasons we urged you to try the tithing attempt. It was a litmus test as to whether these pirates had a hidden agenda. Regular pirates would have taken the tithe, but with their actions the Hezokeen have proven that they were hired as mercenaries.

"And this action also comes too soon after the Eththelnt's last failed attempt at interference on your

148

planet. We believe they were frustrated by its failure and are seeking a more direct line of attack."

"Their last attempt?"

"The Singularity."

Willoch blanched. She had been expecting the Governor to relate some story of covert Eththelnt operations that had been narrowly averted, but—

"The *Singularity?*" she repeated.

"Of course there is only scant evidence of this, but, starting twenty years ago, the Eththelnt began using many corporate and personality fronts to manipulate conditions on your planet to promote singularity-related technologies. They funded the right projects, the right people, and helped smuggle down technologies when necessary, all to create an unstable mix of progress. It was their hand that was behind the AI project in Oslo."

Willoch was reeling.

"But the Eththelnt actually have a poor understanding of singularities—we Lontans are the only experts. So they only succeeded in creating an AI that made an abortive attempt at global domination, and failed. Using the Hezokeen must be their Plan B."

Willoch was still aghast. This discussion of a Lontan–Eththelnt proxy war had all been abstract and high-level, but now she was learning that battles in it had already been fought—and *lost*—by her side. And at such drastic scales ... It made her feel vulnerable, foolish, and blind.

Though there was one strangely positive side effect. Through this she was able to realize that her previous anger at the Lontans had been misplaced. The Governor may have callously announced that the Earth had become the new theater in their war, but that was not by the Lontans' choice. The true blame lay with the Eththelnt. They were the ones fostering dangerous technologies, running front corporations, destroying a city occasionally ... That the Lontans were fighting on the Earth was only because they had to be there to oppose this enemy.

And Willoch could forgive the Lontans their secrecy, as they had only been trying to give the Earth a normal childhood. After First Contact, Humanity could not have faced the future with any alacrity if the Lontans had immediately divulged the truth. If they had whispered into their ears, 'By the way, we and this other species are going to need to fight a proxy war down here. Nothing too extravagant—just a catastrophe every now and then, a cataclysm here and there—you'll get used to it.' The last fifty years of Human history would have played out markedly differently if they had known that up in the heavens was not just a Lontan Governor stewarding their planet, but also an Eththelnt *Anti*-Governor working with completely opposite intent.

"Thank you, Governor," she said—and surprised herself with the words. Indeed she had to repeat them to convince herself that they were not accidental: "Thank you. For all you've told me. The

150

truth I've just learned is ... ugly. But at least we have it in hand."

The Governor nodded. "It was simply time for you to know."

He said this kindly, Willoch thought.

"Though ... " he turned, "there is one last thing I must inform you of. Something we Lontans only just discovered ourselves."

Willoch's gaze sharpened. After the Governor had so casually dropped the truth about the Singularity, the fact that he was warning her of something to come ...

"It stems from our ongoing mission with the ISSO to track down the Hezokeen's planet-side agents," he continued. "During the investigation, we and the ISSO procured some information from deep inside Lindon Securities—you know of this as the corporation behind the corporate army in Norway. This information showed the company's inner workings with conspicuous detail we never had access to before. The people who originally procured it were not ISSO agents themselves, and they interpreted it to mean that Olof Lindon had built some advanced prototype hypercomp system in Oslo.

"With the same facts, however, were we able to make the proper diagnosis. And from it we have learned ... "—here he paused, setting Willoch more on edge—"that the Singularity AI is alive. That it was not destroyed as we had originally thought.

And that it is presently located in the Lindon Securities' superbase in Oslo."

Willoch showed no reaction. This was in stark contrast to the chaos raging inside her. When she managed to speak, it was also with deceptive calm: "The Singularity AI is alive?"

The Governor nodded.

"And Lindon is operating it?"

"Not 'operating it'—quite the opposite, in fact. The AI is now controlling Lindon's company through a massive number of personality fronts. Thousands of them, replacing almost all top officials. Including, apparently, Lindon himself. And it has maintained the illusion of these peoples' existence by vizhacking everyone else in the company. What its ends are we are not sure, but, given the drastic implications of this, we knew we had to share this information with you as soon as possible."

Willoch's mouth had finally fallen open. "And you're *just* finding this out *now?* ... But— ... But you're the Lontans!"

The Governor cocked his head self-amusedly. "True. But the AI was meticulous in concealing its existence. It was obviously trying to hide from us after the failure of its premature awakening. And it had apparently received many advanced technologies from the Eththelnt prior to the Singularity, and it used these to shield itself from detection afterwards.

152

"In fact, even now, we have not directly observed this AI, nor do we have any evidence that this AI *must* be the one from the Singularity. We have only inferred that there is an AI operating in Oslo, and we were able to trace its activity back some four years. So it could be the Singularity AI if it faked its demise, or it could just be a different one created soon afterwards. Given everything else we know, what we have told you is the most likely explanation. But even we are not absolutely certain."

"I assume you're telling us this because you're about to arrest it?" Willoch proceeded strongly. "If the Singularity AI is alive, then you're going to hold it up to charges—just as you assured us you would do five years ago if you ever—"

"Oh, of course," the Governor assured her. "We will certainly hold it to account for the destruction it has caused. Just as soon as you hand it over to us for trial."

Willoch stopped. "Just as soon as *we* ... " She gave a small sigh.

"We Lontans could certainly capture the AI ourselves, but we would have to stage a small invasion of your planet to do so. To get permission for such an excursion we would have to solicit all of your major governments and supranational bodies. By the time we could have assembled all the proper mandates to satisfy Lontan law, you Humans could have moved on the AI much sooner yourselves."

153

'Ahh ... ' Willoch mouthed. So the Lontans were giving them another assignment.

"To which end, we are providing the details in a report to your governments—here is a copy," he sent her a document. "We have already drawn up the necessary warrants for the AI's arrest with the ISSO, though it is hardly likely that the entity will surrender itself willingly. Most likely you will need a military task force to secure the corporate army's superbase and extricate it. We have sketched out the type of attack we believe will suffice."

Willoch leafed through the report and found the outlined military operation. The Lontans had covered all the important angles: the disposition of forces, the technologies that would effectively counter the corporate army, what equipment would penetrate the Bunker, how they could hand over the AI after verifying its existence ...

"I assure you we will move on this immediately," Willoch said. "And I know that the Home Guard will be eager to take the lead in such a task force."

And she suspected that the legal complications the Governor had painted were only a ploy. The Lontans were probably willing to storm the Bunker this minute, but they knew the Humans would have a deep psychological need to do this. Call it vengeance or closure, but they would want to close the book on the Singularity themselves. Willoch had not merely been throwing out bravado when she had mentioned the Home Guard's eagerness. Even if the

Governor had told her that the Lontans would be sacking the Bunker today, Willoch might have said, 'Oh, please, might we do it instead?'

So maybe the Lontans' philosophy was not the *laissez-fairism* she had always suspected. Maybe it was to feign inaction so that the Humans would get used to taking the initiative. As he had said, they had to learn to stand on their own.

"It should take perhaps a week to prepare the attack," the Governor added. "Hopefully by that time the Hezokeen action will have been resolved, but, even if it is not, you may wish to proceed anyway. Knowing that the AI is still alive—and considering what it has done—, we must consider it a threat."

"Indeed," said Willoch. "Even though it's been in hiding for five years, the idea of leaving it alone for another week terrifies me." A troubling possibility struck her, "Wait, you said that the Eththelnt were responsible for creating the AI ... So could they have known it was alive this whole time?"

"Unlikely. They were responsible for its creation, yes, but to them the AI was just a means of touching off a singularity. When it proved a dud, they wrote it off and embarked on this more direct course of action: a pirate razing."

Willoch nodded.

When she was ready to leave, she stood and began walking towards the shuttle. But a few steps away she stopped and looked back.

"I have one last question," she said. "Back when you were talking about the war between you and the Eththelnt, you said the matter of who managed our first contact was the 'opening move' in this new battle. And, since you won, the Eththelnt had to try to kick you out. That's why we're in this predicament.

"But ... if the Eththelnt had won our contract instead ... what would *you* have tried?"

The Governor flickered with a grin. And Willoch grinned slightly back.

Caught you.

The Governor took a breath. "I shall speak plainly. While we abhor the course of action that the Eththelnt have embarked upon ... we would still have done *something*. Yes."

Willoch gave him a steady look. She appreciated this straight answer. He could have simply rebutted or parried the question, but this reply was adult-to-adult. While the Governor could not see the Lontans razing a planet, he could also not vouch for everything that fifty years of desperate war might push them to. Between devils and angels, all he could promise was that they would not be the devils the Eththelnt were.

She turned and left. And, for all the troubling facts she had just learned—all that had become Humanity's burden—, she still felt empowered. Back when the Ambassador had first given them the lead in dealing with the pirate threat, she had thought the Lontans were finally taking them

156

seriously. Now she knew that even then they had been keeping the truth to themselves and were only sending the Humans out on busying errands. But with this meeting they had finally been made equal partners, and they would face the coming crisis with full knowledge of its significance.

Though she did not delude herself that the Lontans had just told them everything. In the years to come there would always be more secrets and revelations—that was inevitable. But with each step they were coming further into their own, becoming more and more a mature and independent people.

Chapter 18 - Plan

One nice thing, Admiral Hadamard thought, about being light-years away from home base and nuzzled up against a superior enemy force, was that good ideas got the attention and turnaround that it usually took a world war to engender.

The perfect example of this was that one Norwegian officer's discovery of the Hezokeen fleet movements. Had Ensign Diesen been an analyst working planet-side, her report would merely have been filed away. But not so out here, where everyone's mortality was tingling them like a persistent itch. Diesen had simply briefed her captain, and then she was off and running up the chain of command. Before an hour was out Hadamard was listening to the same presentation himself, and, once he was convinced, he had forwarded everything back to Fleet and requested a meeting with the Eyes MINDEFs—he would need that level of multinational approval to change their mission objectives. He wanted his ships to scrap the grid and fall back, or perhaps start searching for the displaced Hezokeen fleet.

This meeting was arranged shortly. Going in, Hadamard had expected some resistance from the ministers. Abandoning the grid would be admitting that they had been outsmarted, and then only on the strength of a probability. But, even though Diesen's evidence was shaky, Hadamard was confident in his ability to hammer the facts home. After all, he was not called '"Hard Ass" Hadamard' just because he was French; he was famous for harangues that could put anyone in their cowering place. It was widely accepted that he had been given this sensor grid assignment not only because he was the best man for the job, but also in order to put the insulation of a couple light-years and orders of comm silence in between him and top brass.

Once his meeting with the MINDEFs started, however, he remembered how even hypercomm came with a 6-second round trip delay when casting from 20 light-years out. Every time Hadamard was riveting up into one of his tirades, the comm channel's delaaaaaaaaays ... static!#$%*(!£bursts, and— _ starts and— _ stops—would soon derail him. It was impossible to outmaneuver someone who was already two sentences in the future. Hadamard was hardly even participating in the meeting, rather only yelling back as at some moronic debate on C-SPAN.

He did have some advocates among the audience, but the majority was clearly against him, and they quickly formed a consensus. Hadamard's supposed evidence of Hezokeen fleet movements was statistically unsound, and so it could be rejected out of hand. Yet, even if it held some truth, at most it meant that a fraction of the Hezokeen fleet had escaped. Since the balance of their forces remained in position, Hadamard's task force was to stay put.

Nevertheless, immediately after logging out, Hadamard called his captains and XOs together. Their ships were spread far out, but the simspace meeting was patched together over the sensor grid's ultra-quiet communications mesh.

The CO of the *Saratoga* asked him straightaway, "So how'd the meeting with HQ go, Admiral?"

"A moron clusterfuck," he replied.

Nobody laughed. They had all learned to tell the difference between Hadamard's jocular and sardonic profanity, and this was of the latter kind.

"Downplayed and rejected our intel," he continued. "We're to stay in position while fleet sticks its head in the sand. And they gave me this bullshit about something 'big' coming up Earth-side—something that was more demanding of their attention right now than the possibility of a fucking alien invasion."

When Frisch heard this, he was first shocked ... but then un-shocked. Diesen had moved up the chain of command so quickly that it could only have been *too* quickly—bureaucracy was not meant to work so well. And this turnaround confirmed it: the system had only been toying with them all along.

"—But that's why *we're* taking the initiative," Hadamard interjected. "Fleet was unconvinced by the evidence because they didn't want to be. I gather they only held the meeting because it would give them a chance to tell *me* to go fuck myself for once instead of vice versa. Which means we have to go

160

back out there and get some proof that even they can't shove up their asses." He pounded the table for emphasis, and simspace rendered the effect with such fidelity that it chilled Frisch's spine.

"And here's how we do that," Hadamard's tone turned scheming, and he fired up the tactical holo. "From our first scans we know that the Hezokeen had some five hundred ships in their core. Fleet thinks that, even if our evidence is good, then at most a hundred ships could have made it out, which means that the balance of their forces—and so of our attention—remains here.

"Now, we can't prove them wrong by tracking down the ships that escaped and counting them up. ... But we *can* go *into* the Hezokeen core and count how many ships are *missing*."

The room accepted this with unease. ... Frisch had expected it to be more eloquent and dramatic when he was ordered on a suicide mission.

"Begging your pardon, sir," said Captain Reynolds, "but isn't that suicide?"

"Two reasons why not," said Hadamard. "One is because we're right and the Hezokeen fleet is gone. They left behind only a skeleton force of ships to run laps in hyperspace. Kicking up enough noise to cover for everything that's missing."

Frisch found this unconvincing. The whole point of an incursion into the Hezokeen core was to confirm their intelligence, so to first assume that that intel was correct—and as a matter of life or death—was a dubious contingency.

"And the second reason," said Hadamard, "is because I have a plan."

Frisch liked this one better.

A tactical chart appeared centered on the Hezokeen position. A blue triangle—symbolizing a friendly formation—appeared to one side of it.

"The *Saratoga's* group will form up here and begin demonstrating to make a deep intrusion into Hezokeen space. When they see it, the Hezokeen will think we've seen through their deception. They'll muster their ships to oppose us and try to look as if they had their full strength to bring to bear. If they've left only a skeleton force behind, that should draw in most of what they have.

"But the *Saratoga's* action will be a diversion. Absent from our group will be one destroyer, stationed here." Another blue triangle appeared on the far side of Hezokeen space. "The *Saratoga* will develop her encounter with the Hezokeen, and after fifteen minutes we should have drawn an adequate investment. That's when this destroyer breaks full speed for the Hezokeen core. By the time they see it coming, it'll be too late to screen them.

"Once that destroyer gets far enough inside, it'll sortie dozens of sensor drones. Before those are splashed, they'll have shone a light on the majority of the Hezokeen staging area, telling us definitively what they've left behind. Once that's done, the destroyer makes its escape, and all of our ships rendezvous back at the grid."

The room appraised the plan favorably. It was simple and sturdy, and there was little to dislike—save from the perspective of the crew that would be going on the lone ranger destroyer mission.

Captain Kiergarten cut right to that point by asking, "Which ship is going on the solo mission, sir? Are you leaving it open to volunteers?"

"I thought I might, but it stands to reason that I should send the ship with the greatest chance of making it out unscathed. —I didn't say 'making it out *alive*,' note, because that's not even an issue here—*no one* is dying on this mission. But, still, we're going to be exposed to some real firepower on it, and I don't want any of my ships getting damaged. And it so happens that there's one destroyer in our group that has an advanced hyperdrive capable of short-term boosts into I-band hyperspace."

Frisch saw where this was headed. Under different circumstances, he might have celebrated with an internal exclamation of 'Jackpot!'

"And that's the *Jotunheim*," Hadamard said as his eyes met Frisch's. "Aside from having the ship best-suited to this mission, captain, your crew's qualifications are also exemplary. And I thought they might be eager to see through to completion what they started today with their discovery."

"Of course, sir," Frisch replied. "We wouldn't let you send anyone else." He said this without precisely feeling it. Not that he was afraid of this mission, but he would have preferred to be going on it with more wingmen than just his guardian angel.

"This question is somewhat late, sir," said Reynolds, "but what if you're wrong? What if we'll be flying into the thick of the Hezokeen fleet?"

"I've built in some safeguards for that. That's why the *Saratoga's* group is going in first. If the resistance is too heavy, we send an abort code to the *Jotunheim*, withdraw, and it all ends there. Also, I'm sending the *Jotunheim* in with a full wing of corvettes from the *Saratoga*, plus surplus defense drones. Since those are unmanned they're perfectly expendable, and, with that much insulating firepower, the *Jotunheim* should be able to punch through anything. That work for you, captain?"

Frisch nodded and 'yes, sir'ed back.

"Good. Now, unless there are any glaring travesties outstanding, I want this operation ready to launch in half an hour. It'll take our ships two hours just to get to their ready positions at stealth speeds, so let's not waste any more time before we start paying down that debt. The Hezokeen are probably sitting right outside of the Monitoring Lines at this moment, and yet we're stuck uselessly out here until we can clear up this shit with Fleet. ... Dismissed."

Chapter 19 - Ulterior

Peder returned home from a visit to an antiques store in downtown Stockholm. The shop was a front for the hardware arm of Zuzanna's organization, and Peder had gone to pick up his ghost electron array receivers. He had not known what they would give him, but, upon entering, the clerk had presented him with a 1963 vinyl recording of Prokofiev's Second Piano Concerto. Zuzanna knew he collected LPs, and so the Mafia must have thought one would be a suitable cover for smuggling him his purchase. — And of course they had chosen a Russian composer.

He took the record down to his ASAPR and laid it on his desk. It was missing its original plastic wrapping, but its surface bore only the faintest of hairline scratches and scars. The cover showed the conductor caught at the moment of an orchestral climax, and was stamped overhead with the yellow cornice seal of *Deutsche Grammophon*. The colors were naturally faded—the result of eighty years of oxidation on the pigment technologies of yester-century—, yet this had now wreathed the artifact in hallowed heirloomhood, like the work of a long-dead master painter.

Peder knew the record was not authentic. The Mafia had probably once had the original record in their possession and had made an atomic scan of it, so that they could spin out a nanoconstructed duplicate on demand. What Peder now held was surely one such clone. Yet he was careful in handling it—while strictly a fake, an exact copy of a real record was still worth listening to.

He removed the cover and coaxed the vinyl from its sleeve. It had only been out in the air for a second before his ASAPR began shrieking alarms into his OHUD:

FOREIGN NANOMACHINES DETECTED!
INTERNAL SECURITY COMPROMISED!
INITIATE FULL LOCKDOWN AND
PURGING PROCEDURES? (Y/N)

The record had been dusted with nanomachines—which constituted his true purchase. Once his ASAPR's defensive nanites had detected the material, they had asked for permission to destroy it. They would automatically eliminate any spamware nanomachines, but this exotic and unrecognized technology made them double-check with Peder.

He silenced the alarms and told his ASAPR to disregard the nanites. Then he placed a large sheet of frictionless paper on his desk. He held the record over it and loaded a signal onto his hand chips—one that the Mafia had given him before his trip to the store. He broadcast it, which was supposed to tell the nanites on the LP to cut their molecular bonds and drop onto the paper. He picked the paper up and folded a pouring lip into one side, then decanted the nanites into a programming creche. This work was all delicate make-believe since the nanomachines were invisible to the naked eye. But the programming creche did confirm receipt of the new nanomaterial. He wiped the firmware to a known, clean version, then loaded his communication configuration and cipher material. Then he ran some tests and satisfied himself that everything was in order.

The ghost electron receivers were the means he needed to communicate with his men. And he had gotten final clearance from the Bunker for on-site check-ins with his captains Saturday morning. All he had to do was pass them the receivers.

His only oversight was that he still had no way to do this with them securely. The Bunker did have its own ASAPRs, but those all belonged to Lindon, so everything inside was obviously being recorded so that it could be played back for him later. Peder needed his own ASAPR—a mobile one—, and that would cost him another couple hundred thousand. But this was perfectly in line with the punch-drunk rate he had been spending money that week.

In the middle of his work he received a surprise notification from his house: Zuzanna had arrived. She was at his front door, asking for permission to enter. Peder sent her the okay, and she headed straight for his ASAPR.

Before she arrived Peder scrambled to hide what he was doing. Zuzanna certainly knew about his purchase, but it was simply good practice not to let her see what he was doing with it.

He hurriedly siphoned the programmed nanomachines off into sixteen small vials. He took a cigarette case out of his desk and arrayed the vials inside. This was not really a cigarette case but rather an advanced, active-holographic camouflage container that would appear to be a cigarette case on most sensor modalities no matter what it actually contained. He tucked the case away, then he collected the LP and filed it along with the others he kept in his ASAPR.

Zuzanna entered and saw nothing amiss. After pleasantries and refreshments, Peder said,

"Of course it's nice to have you over, Zizi. But I'm surprised, I thought my last job was over."

"It was—*is*," said Zuzanna. "This isn't about that. It's actually about something ... delicate."

That was the shakiest opening he had ever seen from her.

"I ... need your help."

"Oh?"

She looked down and pursed her lips, searching for where to begin. "You remember ... how I said your last job brought us a little close to the ISSO? ... "

"Yeah ... " Peder leaned forward.

"Well, at the beginning of this week they ... contacted me."

Peder's eyes went wide.

"—Of course you can't let that out," Zuzanna added in a rush.

168

"—Er, no, of course not ... It doesn't sound like something your bosses would be thrilled to hear."

"Right."

"How did they contact you?" Peder was concerned by how much Zuzanna had been exposed and what that meant for him.

"It was secure," she assured him. "They telecast something into my ASAPR while I was alone. Left no trace from the Human angle from what I can tell."

"Well, at least there's that. What did they want?"

"They made me cut a deal to help them. It's all in my bosses' interests, of course. But it's also obviously in *my* interests that they never find out about it."

Peder noted how prudently she was speaking, as if this conversation were being recorded and might one day find its way back to the organization.

"The deal was I gave them everything we uncovered on Lindon from your job. And after that they asked me to lure some contacts out into the open so that they can grab them. I've been making covert inquiries, being as subtle as I can in the time I have. But they sent me after some high-class Japanese racket—I think even Yakuza. So they're not the kind of people you can just drop your business card off with and hope they get back to you.

"To contact them like the ISSO wanted, I had to back off and set up a front. My alias is I'm a Mafia

169

boss who landed some super-hot cargo that I need to smuggle into Japan. And I started making inquiries in such a way that it should eventually get me in touch with the people I want, all while looking entirely convincing. And I'm *close*. I've got a line with some of their low-level gangsters, and I can buy a meet higher up. But the reason I'm here is—"

Peder had been growing anxious for this fact.

"—it's silly, really, but ... I've drained my cash supply. I need to make a few more payments before everything's set up and I'm off the hook with the ISSO, but I'm tapped out. So I ... need some money."

Peder 'ahh'ed.

"I'd pay you back, of course," Zuzanna interjected. "Whatever interest you want. It's just that I'm trying to do this all under my bosses' radar, so I can't liquidate my own assets the way I need to. ... And obviously I *can't* go to the ISSO. They might give me the money, but, just in case my bosses ever found out about this, I don't want to add any exacerbating details to the account. ... And I can't go to my *bosses*, of course ... And I don't trust any of the people I work with or my other clients ... My friends don't have nearly enough ... " She threw her head back, laughing mirthlessly. "And I don't know why I'm here. Asking you. It's not like it's *your* fault. Granted this came from working on your contract, but ... "

That last move was sly, Peder thought. Saying 'it's not your fault' while positing a reason to the

170

contrary, terminated with only an unconvincing, 'but ... ' She knew how to play him.

But he could see why she had come to him: trust was the key. If Zuzanna went to her other wealthy clients, then they might ask for details that she could not share. And, even if they gave her the money, the mere fact of the loan might leak back to her bosses, and then the ensuing questions would put her in an awkward position. But Peder was ideal because her reasons tied in with his last job, so she could count on his discretion. And, in revealing what the ISSO knew about them, she had shown that both their heads were fitted to a noose.

"Ahhh ... " he vocalized, providing a mile marker in his expansive silence.

He was also debating the financial consideration that, with his company about to go bankrupt, he did not have the money to spare Zuzanna one way or the other. But, if the ISSO were on their trail, and they really did have the power to cheat ASAPRs and any other physics at will, then he probably could not afford to *not* pay them off.

"I'm in—of course," he concluded.

"*Thank you,*" Zuzanna said in a way that struck along many dimensions. "Spasibo, spasibo ... " she added in her native language, as if to give it more feeling.

"So how much do you need?" he asked.

"How much do you have?"

171

"Well, I've got an off-planet account with about three hundred k in it."

Zuzanna wavered, but replied, "That should do."

Not picking up on her implication, Peder asked, "Okay, how much will you need?"

"All of it."

"'All of it'?"

"All of it."

... He still did not think he had made his point. "*Allllll.* Of it?"

"Yes. *Trust me,* I'll need every last millicredit."

Shrugging, Peder turned to his computer and pulled up the main page of First Lunar Bank. He logged into his account and worked through the fine mesh of security. At the transfers page he typed in a rounded-off amount while Zuzanna entered her recipient's information. He felt a dread as if he were loading his money into a cannon. He hit the 'Verify' button and proceeded to the final confirmation screen. A pulsing 'Commit' awaited his approval.

He abruptly locked his screen and turned to face Zuzanna. "One condition," he said.

Zuzanna braced for whatever it was.

"If I have this straight," he continued, "you need this money to arrange a meet with the Yakuza. So you lure them out somewhere and the ISSO grabs them; that right?"

Zuzanna nodded.

"Then I'm coming along."

Her expression said she was almost as surprised to hear this as he was himself.

"Why?!" she objected.

An excellent question, thought Peder, posing it to himself. It was because ... this, today, was the first time Zuzanna had come to him as a friend in need. It was fresh and exciting, and he wanted more of it. Still, what was he to do—ask her out to dinner? That would have been ludicrously adolescent under the circumstances. But the only other way he could think to spend time with her was to ask to come along on this venture. So that was why. Zuzanna had cracked the door on a new mode of their relationship, and he wanted to see it forward.

But of course he could not *say* that. So Peder had to come up with an acceptable alternative explanation—a lie.

"Isn't it obvious?" he said. "How can I send you off alone to meet the *Yakuza* while you still owe me three hundred thousand credits? I know you'll pay me back, but I still need to make sure you're alive to do it." He congratulated himself on the success of this concoction.

"Oh ... " said Zuzanna, herself taken aback by such a cogent reply. "Well ... agreed."

Peder committed the transaction.

Zuzanna was gone a minute later, rushing back to work now that she had a refilled slush fund.

And Peder finally felt that there was something bright on his horizon.

173

Chapter 20 - Attention

Late Thursday night in the office, Townsend was playing doubles table tennis with Laake, Mosely, and Zhang. Normally the ISSO was as empty on a Thursday night as any corporate office, but Fleet and the Lontans were insistent that a final Hezokeen action could come 'any day now.' While Townsend was not terribly convinced of that, he did know how moronic he would feel if the apocalypse did come while he was kicking back at home. Many agents were staying late, and his team was taking a break at the game tables.

Mosely made a serve, and Townsend let it bounce past, saying, "I think that was out."

Mosely squinted. "You *think?*"

"There's no 'out' in table tennis serves!" Laake objected.

"Actually, in doubles play," Zhang interjected—him being a natural officiator—, "one has to serve from the right-hand side of the court to the other team's right-hand side."

"And I think the ball was over the centerline," Townsend said.

Mosely frowned. "Again, you *think?*"

"Well the ball bounced right behind a graphic in my viz, so I couldn't see it exactly. What did you guys see?"

"Well, from this angle, the ball bounced right behind that solid part of the net, so me neither," said Laake. "Mosely?"

"Wasn't watching that closely."

Townsend turned to his partner: "All right, Zhang, what was it?"

"I'm sorry, I wasn't paying attention either," he replied.

All three Humans looked at him.

"But can't you just ... scroll back a few seconds and look at the instant replay with those skinjob eyes of yours?" asked Townsend.

"My prime consciousness was actually elsewhere at the time."

"Excuse me?"

"For the purposes of this game, my body was only operating a tertiary consciousness that could manage the table tennis physics competently. When my primary checked back in at the resumption of this discussion, I was updated with only a redacted summary of what had happened previously. There was no play-by-play visual record available, so I did not witness it."

The Humans gave him a bewildered look.

"*Oh*," said Laake. "So you mean *we're* all playing this game, but meanwhile your primary says, 'Fuck these losers, I'm gonna go do something *interesting* instead,' and just leaves behind some dumb shit simulacra to sock-puppet your body and humor us all—is that it?"

This was strong language from Laake—but then his team was losing. And, while Townsend sympathized with him, he stepped in to say,

"What I think Zhang meant to say was 'Do-over.' Serve again."

Mosely sighed. "Okay, but no more of this 'ball's out' shit unless you *see it* next time."

Townsend crouched back into his receiving position.

As Mosely was serving, however, an info alert popped up in Townsend's OHUD. "Hold it," he said, presenting a hand while he scanned the text. The agents had to handle a couple of these pages every hour, so Laake and Mosely paused.

The alert had been generated by a purchase Peder Kjaerstad had made—one that had tripped the 'weirdness' sensors of their data-mining routines. Repeating the details to Zhang, Townsend said,

"Kjaerstad wants an ASAPR installed in his plane by Friday night?"

Zhang pitched in, "Kjaerstad has also scheduled a flight to Oslo for Saturday morning. He must want the ASAPR for extra security for this trip to the Bunker."

"But if he's flying to the Bunker, then why does he need the extra security? His company owns the place—" Townsend caught himself: "Err, *Lindon* owns the place. So no wonder Kjaerstad wants his own ASAPR. Right." Townsend was always on his toes around the mannequin, trying to catch his errors before they became fair game to correct. It was like being on a perpetual job interview representing the Human species.

"It is understandable why Kjaerstad would want extra security," said Zhang, "but installing an ASAPR on his plane—and in a few days—is no paltry expense."

Townsend grumbled. "Once we had Mukhina working for us, I'd just written Kjaerstad off. But this makes me wonder. Obviously he plans to do something in Oslo that he needs to keep hidden from Lindon, but what?"

"Another piece of information:" Zhang added, "yesterday Kjaerstad made a black market acquisition. High cost—nearly a hundred thousand credits."

"What was it?"

"We don't know."

"You don't know?"

"We had him under extensive surveillance before, but it proved excessive and we scaled it back. We just discovered this transaction after the fact, but we were not watching Kjaerstad at the time of the actual exchange."

"... So you weren't paying attention again?" Townsend rephrased.

"Correct."

He sighed forcefully. "I don't get it, Zhang. You're *the Lontans*. Can't you just collect all information everywhere and let some AI sort it out?"

"As you know nothing about our capabilities, you must simply accept my word that that would be impractical."

Townsend grimaced. "Anyway, so Kjaerstad picked up some pricey black market gadget, and now he's flying it to the Bunker under the cover of an ASAPR. Suffice it to say that we should start back up full surveillance on him?"

"Already done."

"That includes seeing inside of his ASAPR tomorrow with your Lontan eyes to find out what this is all about?"

"Of course."

"Good. Then let's get back to the game."

Chapter 21 - Marionette

Erlend was holding a poker game in one of the rec rooms, with Kitano, Ingstad, and Märtha among the players. Being a poker novice, Märtha would normally have been content to coast through the evening as a learning experience. But her petulance was up over Kitano having recently told her that it was time for her to 'move on.' And just when Märtha had been thinking most fondly of how fortunate it had been for her to come to Leknes.

Five years ago she had been orphaned, and up till three months ago she had been stuck in Steigen with her grandfather. Of course she loved her grandfather—with the kind of guilt-extorted, draftee love one always owed their ancestral blood—, but his hometown had been her own Rapunzellesque dungeon. It was all single-minded adults, asinine teachers, and peers who thought of her as the haughty, exiled city girl. She had nurtured many escapist fantasies, but not even the wildest of them had seen her returning to life so totally as she had managed here. She was living in a great city, with a job—of sorts—with the Home Guard, and being shuttled around the country in tanks and jets.

—But now it was time to 'move on.' Märtha's fantasy life was at an end. At least her grandfather had arranged for them to stay around Leknes, but she would be returning to the mundane hell of high school.

So she was intent on using this poker game to extract some vague vengeance against the lot of them. She had downloaded a free OHUD poker coach at the start of the match, and this had been her tireless servitor throughout by analyzing the game history, learning her opponents' strategies, even flagging their tells. And, lest Märtha be overwhelmed by all this information, the program also condensed its intelligence into exact recommendations of play: whether to fold, to stay, or to raise, and by how much. But the strangest thing was she still did not seem to be winning ...

The next hand began. Märtha tapped her 'ante' augspace button and one of her chips flew out from her virtual stack and deposited itself in the pot. Erlend dealt the cards—they were playing with augspace chips, but he demanded they use real cards. When she had asked, he had said it was a protection against hacking. Märtha could understand that, but she had a harder time deciphering the ensuing rituals of 'burn cards' and 'cutting the deck' and just what flimflam they militated against.

"So ... anybody know what was behind that alert at the start of the week?" Märtha asked the group. Her poker coach often recommended that she start a conversation to distract the others.

"Not sure," Erlend replied. "I asked Haze, but he gave me this silence that said, 'You don't wanna know.'"

Lievgarten grumbled. "Well, obviously it had something to do with the alert in space. I heard that the snap drill that Hanssen put us into was ordered by Admiral Willoch. And that things were going ape shit up on Gateway at the time."

"Did you hear anything from your friend on board the *Jotunheim*?" Kitano asked Erlend.

"Nah, she shipped out a week ago. Not a peep since. —Call—."

Märtha 'hmm'ed. "If the alert was from Admiral Willoch, then maybe it was about the pirate fleet?"

"Could be," said Lievgarten. "That's probably how we landed our new assignment of building fallout shelters to guard against the 'intergalactic pirate menace.'" He said this with a bombastic cadence, and the others chuckled.

"But this is serious," objected Märtha. "All the leaders made speeches about the pirates."

Lievgarten huffed. "—Raise ten—Look, all I've seen of these pirates is that telemetry they put on the news a month ago. With the blue dot that was the freighter, and the red dot that was the pirate ship? That's *it*—that's *all* I've seen. And it's hard to get worked up over a *pixel*."

"Hear! Hear!" said Erlend. "But you know what I *am* worked up about? How there haven't been three consecutive quarters of GDP growth since 2040. Let the government do something about that and I'll be ecstatic."

"Right," said Ingstad. "Or get us some single-digit unemployment."

"Wonderful," said Erlend. "Or even a measly tax break—raise five—."

Märtha looked at Erlend with a note of betrayal. She had thought he would be taking this more seriously, given that he was working on the fallout shelters himself.

"That's what a lot of people are saying about the pirates," she said, dejected. "That it's all some ploy to distract us from the economy. But I don't believe it."

"Feh ... " Erlend grumbled dismissively.

After five seconds of silence, Märtha's poker program prodded her to ask another question.

"So where was the Colonel today?" she offered. "I didn't see him around at all."

Erlend took special note of this, wondering whether it signaled a relapse of Märtha's old Hanssen fixation. But at least she was calling him 'the Colonel' now.

"In some mysterious, top-level conference," he answered. "—Raise fifteen—. Secure comms going out all over the world."

"Really?—fold—," said Kitano. "What about?"

"No clue." Though Erlend looked up when he saw Steffens enter the room. "But I'm about to find out ... "

Steffens approached and took her place at the table. Cashing in, she said, "Sorry I'm late, guys. Though it looks like things haven't gotten too far along ... "

"Hold it," Erlend interrupted her. "If you want into this game, it's going to cost you a little more than money."

Steffens gave him a look that contained a vague accusation.

Erlend clarified—a little indignantly—, "*Information* ... Haze's been locked away in secure meetings all day, and you were one of the few people with him."

Steffens looked around slyly. She leaned forward and drew everyone into a conspiratorial circle. "*Well* ... Haze only told me to be *discrete* about it, but not zipper-lipped, you know? I think it was because we were putting together the details on a big operation, and it doesn't help to have something big planned if no one knows about it."

"What was it?" asked Kitano.

Steffens looked back and forth between their captive eyes, savoring the moment. "Well, don't spread this around outside of the field officers yet, but ... we were putting together a plan ... " her voice dropped with every pause, "... to attack ... *Oslo*."

After an appropriate deadpan, Erlend asked, "The corporate army superbase in Oslo?"

"Yeah."

"Oslo, *Norway*, Oslo?"

"The one and only."

He sat back. "That's odd: Hanssen didn't look like someone who was planning a suicide mission."

Lievgarten objected, "And just *where* did Haze get the crazy idea to go after the Bunker?"

"It wasn't his idea—and it wasn't a suicide mission," Steffens answered them both. "The directive came from Admiral Willoch and General Ousland, plus the Norwegian mayors. Apparently Laurantzson hand-picked Hanssen to put it all together."

Erlend whistled in astonishment. "—Raise ten—," he said. Those still in the game were confusedly drawn back in.

Steffens continued elaborating over the final round of betting: "Haze told us we were supposed to come up with a plan to crack the superbase in terms of tank divisions and fighter squadrons, no matter where they came from. In the end we needed something like three times the Home Guard forces alone."

"Ahhh, so that's what all those world-wide secure comms were for? Going on a pledge drive to the other militaries?"

"Yup. Confederation and Russian units for sure. Maybe some from the States, too, though they mostly just have special forces around Europe these days."

In the ensuing pause, Erlend nudged Märtha. She had forgotten that the last round of betting had ended to her. On her poker coach's advice, she called, pitching in the requisite chips.

They turned over their cards: Märtha had made two pair while Erlend had three of a kind. The table tallied him the winner, and the pot's chips went flying into his own stacks.

"A little advice:" he said, leaning towards Märtha, "quit the game engine—you're playing like a zombie."

Märtha chagrined. But closed the program.

Chapter 22 - Spearhead

The *Jotunheim* was treading slowly through hyperspace. The surrounding volume was quiet and taut, like the surface of a still pond. The ship was continually reducing speed as she encroached on the Hezokeen position, turning her wake into an even fainter ripple on that medium.

And Frisch could feel the ship tense beneath him. The vessel was an organism, and Frisch could read her state just as a rider who had learned to interpret the moods of his horse. Right now she was as tense as a bowstring, ready for the mission ahead. Not that they had 'told' the ship its mission, but her artificial intelligence could deduce the obvious. They had optimized her for speed, given her a large number of escorts, and crept up to a point dangerously close to the Hezokeen staging area, facing inwards. The next order they gave was hardly likely to be a 'Never mind.'

By the mission clock, the *Saratoga's* group had started its incursion into Hezokeen space twelve minutes ago, so in three minutes the *Jotunheim* was due to light off on a sprint of her own. Before then, Hadamard could always send the abort signal: 'Too many Hezokeen; fall back and regroup.' But Frisch knew that would not happen. In space combat, unequal battles were often resolved with the celerity of a game of nine ball. If the *Saratoga's* group had kept the Hezokeen busy for twelve minutes, that meant they were evenly matched, and they could easily hold out for three more.

Another Hezokeen patrol was just moving out of sensor range. The *Jotunheim's* crew had been listening to such enemy patrols pace distantly for the last half hour. All had passed them by, unaware of their stealth approach.

Even though the bridge only seated five officers, the *Jotunheim's* entire crew was logged into tacspace to follow the intrusion. There was no general quarters that required them to be up, and in fact many of them were slated to be in their bunks—to be fresh for the next crew rotation. But the mortal danger involved in this mission would have kept Frisch from sleep, too.

Despite everyone being awake, there was not a whisper being exchanged on thoughtwave. Not even from any private conversations that everyone could at least sense the ripples from. Frisch often felt like offering a brief, reassuring word to his officers, but the intense quietude seemed to demand it stay undisturbed.

With sixty seconds to go, the ship warmed her engines and prepared her power conduits for maximum throughput. Tacspace showed their planned intrusion course: a corkscrew series of randomized maneuvers designed to minimize their chances of being intercepted and screened. They would have to blaze through hyperspace for 159 seconds before reaching the Hezokeen core. Then they would launch their buoys and it would take another 140 seconds to fight their way across to the *Saratoga*.

The countdown broke thirty seconds ...

10 seconds ... 9 ... 8 ...

In the elongated timesense of tacspace, the seconds really were taking longer than usual.

5 ... 4—

«That's close enough» preempted Frisch. He gave the command and the ship sprang forward, with her escort corvettes spurring after the premature launch.

Their engines stamped a sonic boom into hyperspace that swept away all of their tedious stealth. The mission clock knew to jump to positive time, that it was now counting the seconds of their headlong charge: +1, 2, 3 ...

Their speedometer surged and they quickly cleared the Factor 1 speeds—the domain of freighters and commercial vessels. Seconds later they blazed past Factor 2 and entered the realm of solely military capability. Their speed kept climbing by fractions, but quickly met diminishing returns.

«ENG: Engines peeking» Kittelsen reported. «Factor 2.75 ... // 2.85 ... // 2.93; maxed out»

Their top speed was theoretically better than anything the Hezokeen could reach. But there was a tradeoff to this, and it lay in how, the faster a ship went in hyperspace, the worse its sensor resolution became. Once past Factor 2 their forward vision began shrinking until the *Jotunheim* was effectively blind. Yet meanwhile she had become astonishingly

188

visible to the Hezokeen, since the *Jotunheim* was now at the prow of a javelin wedge of turbulence thundering through their space. The entire enemy fleet would know where they were, and so any second would bring the first attempt to intercept them.

Hence Bruun announced, «NAV: Performing first evasive»

Frisch watched the engine stats. Kittelsen put their reactor into the red, ramping briefly up to 115% for a burst of speed up to a blistering 2.97. They held this over-throttling for only a second before ramping back down to 60% for emergency cool down; then they changed course and shot back up to 100% along a new vector. This sent a tsunami of turbulence thundering ahead along their old course while masking their correction for as long as possible.

A second later a salvo of Hezokeen missiles came streaking in. These approached obliquely from the sides, however, and were easily splashed by the *Jotunheim's* defenses. This meant that the nearest Hezokeen had been thrown by the evasive maneuver. Otherwise, the missiles—or a ship itself—would have come from ahead, leaving critically little time to respond.

«Well, we made that dodge fine» said Khlebnikova, sounding half hopeful.

Frisch concurred. «Though I doubt this computer-optimized course will get us all the way to the core» he added. So far they had not touched a control on their ship besides the 'Go' button; everything had been pre-programmed.

Driving deeper into Hezokeen space, an increasing density of missiles began harassing them from the sides and stern. The number of inbounds would crescendo slowly, the angles of attack would creep forward as the Hezokeen cinched in ... — Then the *Jotunheim* would perform another maneuver and shake the pursuit a little looser. Their blinded sensors could never see any of the enemy ships, but, thanks to their speed advantage, they knew the Hezokeen had to be falling behind them like enraged linebackers chasing a runaway receiver.

After a full eighty seconds along their intrusion, Frisch could confidently say, 'We were right.' The balance of the Hezokeen fleet was gone and they had left only this skeleton force behind. Otherwise the only way the *Jotunheim* would have made it this deep would have been as a hail of debris coasting on momentum alone.

A Hezokeen ship appeared dead ahead, diving across their bow—a destroyer. A thicket of a hundred missiles preceded it, and the enemy ship was paying out ever more shots as she augered in. Both ships were pulling max velocity so they would joust past each other at a dizzying speed.

Frisch ordered, «CO: Break to port / full countermeasures / max fire response»

The *Jotunheim* put out an answering wave of interceptors, and her corvettes rotated forward to momentarily bolster her defenses.

«That's a reckless maneuver» said Khlebnikova, commenting on the Hezokeen attack. «We have over a dozen escorts, but they have nothing»

«They must think we're too busy producing anti-missiles to have the spare resources to shoot back» said Koltsov.

«Enlighten them» ordered Frisch.

The *Jotunheim* did not have the nanossembler throughput to produce both enough countermeasures to protect herself and enough missiles to kill the Hezokeen ship. Which was why the ship had previously built up a stockpile of warheads in her forward launchers. Koltsov now simply asked for a firing solution and opted to expend eighty missiles, which would buy them a 90% chance of splashing their target.

The two ships crossed with each paying out a blizzard of warheads. The *Jotunheim* saved her heaviest blow for just as the Hezokeen was passing point-blank. Her attack quickly saturated the enemy's defenses, and so many missiles slipped through that that '90%' estimate turned out to have been superbly conservative.

All hyperspace warheads had two stages, necessitated by the fact that it was impossible to damage a ship that was inside of its own universe bubble. Thus the first stage was a hyperdisruptor that knocked the ship and the missile back to the real universe. The second stage was the plain explosive that attempted to destroy the ship the old-fashioned way back there. But, while distances contracted going into hyperspace, they dilated while coming back out—and also accumulated a large amount of dither. No matter how close the missile and the ship had been in hyperspace, once both appeared back in the realverse that distance might suddenly have become a light-second across. Even if the missile then erupted with a multi-Gigaton explosion, the target might see it as nothing more than a distant firework. A lucky ship might be saved by just this quirk even when several missiles pierced its defense screens.

But this chance did not exist when dozens of warheads slipped through. The first few missiles might be thrown by the hyperturbulence, but those that piled in later could detransit at leisure, landing right atop the target. When that much raw, space-boiling energy was brought to bear against a tin can in space, even the best shields and armors counted for nothing.

The crew of the *Jotunheim* could not see the Hezokeen ship's destruction directly, but, when it dropped out of hyperspace, and thirty missiles detransited over its last known location, it was obvious what was happening space-side.

The crew celebrated unanimously.

«I think that showed 'em» commented Koltsov.

«They won't try a dead-on charge again» added Bruun.

Frisch alone remained reserved, as he thought a captain should be. But inwardly he was also struck by the significance of possibly being the first Humans to kill any aliens. If Hadamard's intrusion had scored no hits of its own, then the *Jotunheim* had just made the first ship-to-ship kill in Human history. They may have only been doing their jobs, but there was a real stigma to murder. Human mythology had even invented the parable of Cain and Abel to give a face to so terrible a concept. Yet in this new class of murder there would be no doubt about its inaugurators: 'Frisch the Xenocide and the crew of the *Jotunheim*.'

The next minute of their incursion was met by no more such reckless attacks. Missiles hammered them constantly from the back and the sides, and they eventually lost one, then two, then four of their escort corvettes. But these were unmanned and so had been expendable from the beginning. There was nothing fierce enough to deter their progress.

Though, once they were 20 seconds away from the core, Frisch knew they were heading into an ambush. The Hezokeen might have been unsure about their destination at the start, but now all of the *Jotunheim's* random course changes were averaging out. So Frisch told his crew to ready their escape maneuver:

«CO: NAV – prep for I-band boosting // ENG – it's gonna be one of those 'gimme all she's got' moments soon»

Kittelsen and Bruun made their preparations.

In six seconds his prediction came true: their forward screens became saturated with an astounding density of missiles. The *Jotunheim* would be destroyed with even more outrageous overkill than their Hezokeen victim. Their only chance at an evasive maneuver was to brake terrifically and veer away. This would at least reduce the closure rate of the missiles and give the ship a little more time to produce countermeasures. But it would do nothing to change their fate.

So Frisch flashed the 'go' command.

Kittelsen said, «Boosting» and the *Jotunheim's* hyperdrive shifted them up another band in hyperspace, from Ib to I.

The immediate effect was that their tactical screens were wiped clean. Just as the hyperverse was distinct from the regular universe, so was every band of hyperspace distinct from every other. The *Jotunheim* and the Hezokeen missile salvo had been in the commonly used Ib band, but, once the *Jotunheim* boosted up a level, she was in a vacant frontier. And, thanks to the mechanics of hyperspace, she was also moving e times faster than before.

The caveat was that I-band boosting came at the price of running their hyperdrive at almost

300% capacity, and no reactor could long sustain such output before ceasing to be a 'reactor' and becoming a plain 'explosion.'

Just before their drive flashed over, safety overrides shunted them back to Ib band. Maintenance was rushed onto all engine systems to keep them running at merely 100%. They had sustained the boost for 1.477 seconds, which saw them reappear on the far side of the Hezokeen missile salvo, cleanly evading them all.

«WEPS: Salvo cleared / no chance for kill»

But the Hezokeen knew about I-band boosting, and they knew that no modern ship could sustain it for long. Thus, when they had seen the *Jotunheim* blink away, they fired a second missile salvo in advance of them. As soon as their quarry reappeared, those dispersed warheads re-vectored for them. Koltsov's voice soon had to race:

«WEPS: Second salvo detected / missiles converging / overwhelming weapons lock»

«NAV: Hezokeen ships to starboard, gallant, forward / on approach»

Khlebnikova ordered an evasive, but they had reappeared in the middle of the Hezokeen wall of ships. They had escaped one noose only to be fitted to another.

So Frisch made a quick decision—the only decision. He waited till just before they were about to be destroyed, then ordered, «CO: Boost again // Reverse evasive to starboard gallant»

Again the reactor surged super-critical and they jumped into the vacancy of I-band. Last time they had charged into and leapfrogged over the missile salvo, so, hoping that the Hezokeen expected the same this time, he ordered the opposite maneuver: veer away and stretch the distance. This time their ragged engines could only sustain the boost for 0.696 seconds. When they transited back to I♭ band—

«Oh hell—» said Frisch.

Their maneuver had been so unexpected that they reappeared nearly abreast of a Hezokeen destroyer, closing rapidly. The two ships veered away from collision—but still had the presence of mind to shoot at each other. They exchanged fire with the cudgeling disputation of two ships of the line, until they opened up a safe distance between them, no damage to either side.

Frisch knew they would get little more out of boosting again—if the ship could even manage it. When he checked the engines, the option to boost was even disallowed, as apparently trying it again would be equivalent to hitting the ship's self-destruct button. The engines demanded at least eleven seconds to recuperate.

But they had cleared the Hezokeen barricade. There was another swarm of missiles encroaching from the back and sides, but their point defenses could narrowly handle those.

«CO: We're here to stay: / sortie new defense screens» Frisch ordered.

Boosting to I-band had left not only the Hezokeen behind but also the *Jotunheim's* own escort corvettes and defense platforms, which were incapable of the same maneuver. The ship now had to deploy replacement drones to rebuild her protective valence.

«XO: Deploy the probes // Hit the escape course» ordered Khlebnikova.

The ship's launch ports paid out the hundred-odd sensor buoys that were the crux of her mission. These irised out in a bouquet of vectors, pinging away and streaming the telemetry back to Hadamard's group. A few of the drones were splashed immediately, and the Hezokeen even directed their next missile salvo at these probes instead of at the *Jotunheim*. But the balance of them went climbing unstoppably outwards, shining a light on the entire Hezokeen position. They had accomplished their mission.

—Or at least everything except for the 'getting out alive' part.

Towards that end, the *Jotunheim* received a coded burst from the *Saratoga* that outlined a rendezvous course for both groups. They only had to follow another series of randomized maneuvers, corkscrew turns, and blistering speed runs before they could safely rejoin the fleet. But Frisch knew that that would be easy. They had already left the balance of Hezokeen ships behind.

Chapter 23 - Conspiracy

Inside of his jet ASAPR, Peder Kjaerstad stood and shook hands with Žigić, one of his corporate army captains.

"Well, it was ... good seeing you again, sir," said Žigić in parting.

"The same," replied Peder. "—Glad to see you and your men doing so well."

Žigić needed take but one step to enter the ASAPR's vestibule. The screen shut behind him and he began to cycle out through the many layers of security.

Once alone again, Peder flopped back in his chair with a sigh.

He recalled all the expenses he had incurred this week. First, the hefty sum to procure sixteen ghost electron comm arrays from the Mafia, one for each of his captains. Second, the payout to Zuzanna to fund her activities and keep the ISSO off of their tails. And third, the unholy exorbitance of having an ASAPR rush-installed on his jet in time for this trip to Oslo. All this so that he might come to the Bunker and enlist his captains in a conspiracy ... and he had just let three of them come and go without doing anything.

Though he quickly realized his error. To get here had only cost money, but to actually convince his men to follow him—or to even broach the topic—would require building a solemn air of trust with each. It was akin to soliciting support for a mutiny: he had to keep the dialogue always circumspect and hypothetical, speaking through a gradually lifting veil of innuendo, until— ... Only now did he realize what delicacy this would take, yet he had not even thought to practice these interviews beforehand. So here he was on opening night, not just unrehearsed in the script, but improvising his part entirely.

The interview with his first captain had been curiously awkward. Fifteen minutes of skirting no issue in particular until he finally let the man duck out. Though Peder had honestly not expected to break through on his first try, and so he excused himself that failure. Yet then his second interview— and now his third with Žigić—had gone just the same. Now he had thirteen interviews left but still sixteen unused nanovials.

Peder checked the schedule to see who was the next captain he would receive ... Erik Mohr. Mohr was one of those who had been with Peder's company from before the Lindon days, back when they were plain high-class corporate security. Peder could still remember Mohr's interview back in '38. Mohr confident in his abilities, yet, like so many military men, averse to having to sell them. He recalled Mohr saying something along the lines of, "From my resume you know I've got experience. And from this interview you know I'm not one of those broken-down, 'The horror! The horror!' types. So do you really need the answers to all the bullshit

199

motivational questions like how I plan to grow as a beautiful little snowflake at your company?" ... Yes, Peder searched his LifeLog and found that quote from Mohr, plus or minus five percent.

A minute later Mohr cycled into the ASAPR. He was sweaty and dusty—apparently Atkins was keeping the men too busy to even change before seeing him. Mohr gave a cramped look around the small room, which had space for only two chairs. He took his seat, and the chairs were so close together that they had to sit angled to keep their knees from hitting.

"Please forgive the cramped accommodations," Peder opened with. "I just had this ASAPR installed, and I wanted to break it in."

"Quite all right, sir," said Mohr. He cleared his throat.

"... Lindon was a little irate about me bringing my own ASAPR," Peder continued in that vein. "He said the Bunker had plenty of those itself. But I insisted on this one. ... I suppose he doesn't like anything happening in his company that he doesn't have perfect knowledge of."

"Ah, true, sir. In fact, just outside I saw a SIGINT truck pulled up next to your jet. Atkins must have the men trying to hack in."

Peder went slightly wide-eyed.

"—As an exercise," Mohr added.

"Ah, yes ... " Peder chuckled to hide his unease. Though he was actually terrified of the massive hypercomp cluster he knew Lindon was running in the Bunker. Yet ASAPR security was still based on physical laws, so it was theoretically proofed against even infinite computing power.

"... And I hope you forgive my insistence on an ASAPR," Peder continued, still trying to break the ice. "I know this must seem like going overboard. None of the other CEOs use them for their one-on-ones."

"That's all right, sir," said Mohr. "Actually, I wish more of the brass would take security this seriously."

Peder cocked his head. "Oh?"

Mohr squirmed—he had been a little too candid with that. He backpedaled, "Well, that was ... just an impression."

But Peder held to his apprehensive look. He was grasping for anything to start a conversation.

Mohr gave in: "It's just something I picked up on during the fight with the Home Guard. They had such good intel on us—I mean crazy-good—that I started thinking we should be using ASAPRs for everything."

"Really?" Peder was genuinely curious. All he knew about the Home Guard War was what he had seen in the biweekly briefings with Lindon. He had been incredulous that the corporate army could be losing so badly, but he had simply accepted it. This was the first he had heard of any intelligence failure on their part.

"Back then, my main assignment was to help protect convoys we were running to the outlying bases. And there were several times when we were hit by these really deep ambushes."

"'Deep' as in ... 'complex'?"

"No, just deep within our territory. I mean, there were the few high-profile losses where we sent convoys way too far out into the country—like the E-10 job. But the balance of our losses actually came from lots of smaller, undefended convoys being destroyed well within our borders. The chances that the Home Guard would have known where they were, and that they'd be able to infiltrate that deep, and then get back out again ... Well, by the end it had happened just a few too many times to be believable."

"Uh-huh ... " Peder mulled, and pretended to be jotting down something in his OHUD. In reality the only higher-up he had to go to with these suspicions was Lindon, and he had no reason to do that. But he did not want to appear powerless in front of Mohr, so he played at taking notes.

During Peder's pause, Mohr inserted a question of his own, "So ... what exactly are these interviews for, sir?"

Peder looked up. "What are they for?"

None of the previous captains had asked this. They had all interpreted them correctly as another pointless bureaucratic exercise. Their ex-CEO was coming in for some face time with his captains—must be part of a union contract somewhere. Mohr would surely know that. But by asking he was almost holding Peder to account for the waste. 'You and I both know that this is all nonsense, but I want to hear you say it.' Peder remembered this forthrightness being one of Mohr's trademarks.

'What are they for?' Peder repeated to himself ... Because, in turning the words over, he had found the perfect opportunity to open up in confidence to Mohr.

"What are they for—honestly?" he said aloud. "They're a power play. Three months ago, I had to hand over control of all my men—all of *you*—to Lindon. He'd already taken over most of the day-to-day operations, but with this I had to surrender all of my command codes and comm channels. After that there was no way for me to reach any of you without going through him. And all the other CEOs had done this long before. But Lindon had promised me that, even though he'd cut me out, I'd still be allowed 'periodic access' to you. But he gave me nothing. So this week I finally went to him and demanded that I get my ... 'period.'"

They both grinned at the unintended joke.

"And so now here I am. No complaints I hope? You and your men being taken care of?" He said this in slight self-mockery, realizing how much he sounded like a Red Cross inspector touring a POW camp.

"No. No complaints, sir," Mohr replied. "Though ... I have to say ... not all of us are ... okay with the circumstances out here."

Peder gave him a prompting gesture.

"It's hard to explain, sir ... " Mohr glanced upwards. "A lot of us look around and ... wonder how we got here. In the middle of Oslo. Inside some gigantic base we haven't seen the likes of in vids ... And that was already strange enough, but now this week they have us carpeting the city with mines and putting SAMs in nearly every building. They say it's to ward off a Home Guard attack—for the isolation drill starting soon. But we've put enough SAMs out there to shoot down the entire Chinese Air Force, and it's hard to believe in *that* level of overkill."

For Mohr, this was the first time he had shared these suspicions with anyone. Perhaps because this was the first time he had had privacy and a sympathetic ear since arriving in Oslo. And yet he did not *know* Kjaerstad, and he had no reason to trust him beyond a little shared animosity he had revealed towards Lindon. The fact that he was opening up so quickly was an admission of how much the situation was bothering him.

Mohr continued, "The men in my unit ... sometimes we ask each other what's going on. And we try to reason it through. But we always end up having to joke it off. Because there's no answers we can come up with. And making jokes is the only thing we can do. But we all know that, somewhere, the jokes have to stop.

"And actually, sir, I was hoping you could tell me what's going on. Something that I could take back to the boys and say, '*Here's* what this is all

204

about.' Because we've tried to roll with it, and it's rattling us."

Peder had maintained an understanding mask while Mohr spoke, but all the while he was thinking what a perfect angle this presented him. He had failed to break through to his other captains, but with Mohr it was like planets aligning.

He dropped his voice earnestly to say, "Actually, Captain, I'm even less in the know than you are. When we handed over control to Lindon, he cut us *completely* out of the loop. So, while neither you nor I have any idea of the man's grand design, at least you're on the front line. You know what Lindon's ordering you to do from day to day. I only just learned about the mining and the laying of SAMs from meeting with Žigić. So, as to what Lindon really means it all for ... " he opened his hands.

Mohr nodded in a dejected way. He had not truly expected an explanation.

"But," Peder turned, "while the other CEOs may have accepted being shut out, I haven't. And I didn't come down here just to get a small concession out of Lindon. Some days I stop and think—like you—, 'How the hell did I end up here?' I thought I had it all laid out when I set up a corporate security firm. I had some high-level contracts; business was growing; I was set. But then I accepted just the wrong job from this guy named Olof Lindon, and now look where we've all ended up."

Mohr felt a mix of reassurance and unease at these words. The former because here was his commander, voicing his same concerns, in words and sentiments so closely mirroring his own. And the latter for precisely the same reason: here was his *commander* confessing that his ignorance was even deeper. This last week, Mohr had been holding on to the hope that the Oslo mess at least made sense from a higher perspective. Kjaerstad's words had stripped him of that hope, but, wherever that left him, it was at least on solid ground.

"What I'm about to say is the reason I came down here in my own ASAPR," Peder continued. "Several months ago I started an investigation into Lindon and the company. —And I contracted this from the Russian Mafia, so I wasn't playing around. And, in the course of it, I discovered some facts that were ... hard to explain. It didn't tell me what Lindon was planning, but it made me wonder even more what he meant to do with the army and his base here. Yet I was out of the loop and had no way of finding out.

"But that didn't matter. Because I was still responsible. Responsible for the men I put in Lindon's hands, and for what he does with them. So I came down here with a way to put me—and you— back in the loop."

Mohr's eyes were cool, his expression flat. From there shone no judgment yet. He was still listening.

"All it is is a comm." Peder took one of the nanovials out of his pocket and held it up to Mohr. "A nanoarray that will be able to receive signals even when it's inside of the Bunker. Something that you can conceal on your person. It's only ... a failsafe. A hotline between me and you. I already gave this to some of the other captains and they accepted." He imagined this small lie would help grease the treads.

He proffered the vial. Mohr waited some seconds before reaching towards it.

"That's a ... simple request," he said. "Though ... even after all we've just said, I can't imagine when this would actually be necessary. Granted the situation is strange, but, when you get down to it, what *could* Lindon be doing?"

Peder nodded. "You're right. For all my suspicions, I always find myself falling back to saying, 'But, honestly, what *could* Lindon be up to that's so dangerous?' That's a normal impulse.

"But we are not in a normal situation here. We work for the only man on the planet with a private army, a massive base on international territory, and no legal strings tying him down. That might be okay if he were forthright and open about everything, but he's the exact opposite.

"Lindon's breaking some heavy laws, and there are organizations that know this—and that are watching him right now. They seem to be looking the other way for the moment, *or* they might just be building up enough evidence before they act. But

207

some day an ISSO or Confederation Police task force will kick over every brick of Lindon Securities, and a great number of people are going to jail. The only ones who'll escape are those who didn't simply go with the flow that led to all of it. Now I don't know if this"—he gestured at the vial—"will be enough to pardon us. But it's a start.

"And, even though I can't say what Lindon is planning, the mere fact that you and I have been brought to this—that we're even considering this—is the reason why it's necessary."

Mohr turned the vial over. He was thinking how small and how great a thing it was. At face value it was only a communications device, and taking it was nothing more than a little insurance. But Lindon and Atkins had done their utmost to isolate the men from the outside world, and so to break through that curtain would be labeled 'sedition' and 'conspiracy.'

And, ultimately, that was what convinced him. If everything were fine, then Lindon and Atkins would not care about something as innocuous as this comm array. But the fact that they would meant that Mohr had to as well. And so he knew his course.

He closed his fingers over the vial in an accepting grip. "Okay. What do I do?"

Peder nodded. "Put it over the back of your wrist and break it."

Mohr placed it over his left wrist and pushed down. The capsule broke easily, and a thin film of nanosludge slid out. He brushed off the capsule shards and the sludge suffused his skin, leaving no visible trace.

"That's it," said Peder. "The nanites will build an antenna there, about the size of a fingerprint. They'll stay blended imperceptibly in with your skin. If they ever receive a message, the surface will become slightly rough. Then you can download the packet through your hand chips."

Mohr felt the patch of skin, finding it no different. "You said that you gave this to some of the other captains?"

Peder nodded.

Mohr knew not to ask their names. For him to approach any of them outside would be as good as surrendering to Atkins—who would certainly be watching them all closely after these jet ASAPR meetings. And asking Kjaerstad who they were would only look suspicious, as if he were planning to turn them in. He might assume that they were the captains whom Kjaerstad had spoken to already that day, but he could not be sure.

After a pause, they both stood.

"As a final word," said Peder, "I've told no one else about this array. So if you receive a message it will come from me personally."

Mohr nodded. "And, as *my* final word ... I hope I never receive a message on this channel, sir."

Shaking hands, Peder answered, "I hope I never have to send one."

Chapter 24 - Perigee

Once Hanssen had finished his inspection of Camp Aerlig, he strolled alone out to the far end of the tarmac and stood staring southeast. Under the autumn sunset, that was the first darkening part of the sky, where night was gaining purchase. The direction of Oslo.

Since leaving that city five years ago, this was Hanssen's point of closest approach to it. Indeed, every step he took towards it became his new closest approach, and his feet seemed not to want to stop. He only halted where the plascrete tarmac ended and gave way to grass. And there he stood, staring on the distant scene.

Back when they had agreed to the corporate army's proposed withdrawal to Oslo, Hanssen had not known how much it would disgust him. He had told himself that the city was already in enemy territory, so 'handing it over' was not even a symbolic act. But it was. And a deep desecration. The city should have been reclaimed and turned into a hallowed memorial, but instead they had written it off as a bad debt. It was no longer 'Oslo' but the property of the Lindon Multinational Securities Corporation. 'Lindonland' the men were calling it— like some theme park for the world's super rich. Hanssen could imagine the strident ads himself: 'Come to Lindonland! Ride shotgun in a hovertank!

Play target practice with downtown Oslo! Come soon before there's nothing left!'

But that would end soon. He had been stunned when Admiral Willoch ordered a plan to attack the city. For a while he even thought he had imagined it. But all the conferences he had had with generals and ministers from around the world had confirmed it: the attack was real. Next week, the militaries of a dozen countries would converge on Norway. They would charge into Oslo, storm Lindon's superbase, and root out the thing responsible for the Singularity. They would finally close the book. Maybe then those millions of souls would be at rest.

He spurred around and walked back to base. He was anxious to get away, to recede from this perigee. He met up with Erlend and they were soon rocketing out on a wave of turbulence, returning to Leknes.

Airborne, Erlend asked him, "You want to give the border one last buzz on the way out?"

Hanssen said nothing, but he secretly bridled at the whole concept of having 'borders' with the corporate army. Erlend took his silence as tacit consent, however, and detoured east.

Camp Aerlig was one of the new, forward Home Guard outposts that had been planted around corporate army territory. And, for every new HG post, there was a mirroring Lindon one. Thus the two sides were always within a short, antagonistic lurch of each other.

Visualizing the border in an OHUD pane, Erlend saw a jagged line marring the ground and extending upwards as a transparent, semi-infinite wall. He could see exactly where the Home Guard's airspace ended and Lindon's began—and so he knew exactly how many meters of proximity he could dare before provoking an official incident.

Once Erlend had veered within a foot of such, they received comm activity from the other side:

"Lindon Securities post 17 to unidentified Home Guard flight, please respond." The voice was flat and computerized, masking the identity of the speaker. The hail repeated.

"Lindon Securities post 17," Erlend responded, "this is Home Guard flight 69; what can I do ya for?"

Erlend's voice transmission had been given the same neutering signal processing, but it could not mask his peculiar speech patterns. Of course it was unwise to speak this way. If the corporates could identify him, and if they knew that he usually flew Colonel Hanssen around, then they might risk 'accidentally' shooting him down. Scoring such a coup of an assassination would be worth any merely diplomatic fallout.

"Looks like you're giving the border a close shave there," the soldier replied.

"Nothin' wrong with that, I hope."

"Nah. ... You want us to fire some interceptors? Give you some real exercise?"

"Sure. If you don't mind wasting a few missiles."

"Yeahhh, fuck it. Have a nice day. Post 17 out."

"Flight 69 out." To Hanssen he commented, "Got some nice, regular guys over there."

Hanssen was looking distantly out the window. The flare of the setting sun was saturating the left side of the cockpit.

"So ... " Erlend said some minutes later, "I think we gotta send the ANP packing, Haze."

Hanssen turned to focus back on him. He sighed. "They'll be gone in a week or so."

"Not soon enough."

Hanssen could tell that Erlend was prodding him to prod him back. "Any reason in particular?" he obliged.

"Well, you know me, I see conspiracy lurking everywhere," Erlend first gave a disclaimer. "*But* I've been turning this over in my suspicion engine for a good while now, and I think I've come up with something. It's about the ANP's intel.

"You see ... they came to us at the start of this campaign, demoed their stuff, and it was great. And that sorta made sense: drug money trumps every other kind of money—even corporate behemoth money. Even *Lindon* money. But they admitted that their intel war with the corporates had its ups and downs. They showed us their history, and, every month or so, the advantage flipped back to the other side. When they came to us, it just so happened that the ANP was winning. That was all fine.

213

"But, once we started blowing shit up, you might have expected Lindon to invest seriously in getting the advantage. I know every day I was expecting the ANP's intel net to suddenly go dark, and then that'd be the end of the campaign. Yet that never happened. Whatever Lindon and the corporates tried, the ANP managed to stay on top for the entire campaign? It doesn't seem right."

Hanssen shrugged. "There are plenty of ways to explain that. Maybe both the corporates and the ANP geared up once the campaign began, so, since the ANP started out on top, they just rode it all the way through. ... Or maybe the ANP has a spy inside Lindon that they used this time. ... Or maybe they were holding some technologies in reserve. Plenty of explanations. Even though they didn't share the details with us, that doesn't prove it was something bad."

"Yeah, sure, I thought of all that," said Erlend. "But think about this scenario. Say ... it's a week or so into the campaign. Lindon rolls out some new security technology and suddenly it's lights out for the ANP. And now the ANP has the choice of throwing in some reserves—like you think they might have—*or* of just coming back to us and saying, 'Sorry, the corporates won. Everything's shut down. Game over.' Then they can get back to their drug-running and pull their men off the line. This probably happened, even if behind the scenes, right?

214

"Yet, when it did, they actually acted in good faith to keep their agreement? They threw in their strategic reserves to help us, *the Home Guard?*" his tone peaked in incredulity. "But you know the ANP. I mean, sure, there are a few guys in it like Ingstad whom I *wouldn't* kill. But everything else is rotten. And I'm supposed to believe in this glorious, altruistic scenario? No way. Nuh-uh."

Hanssen nodded slowly. Erlend did have a point. ... An obfuscated one, yes, but not without merit. There must have been many opportunities where the ANP could have folded up its operations, but they had passed them by. Even now that the campaign was officially over, the ANP was still on board.

"Okay," Hanssen granted him. "But, even if they have some ulterior motives, they've had weeks to screw us over and they haven't."

"I know, I know ... " grumbled Erlend. "Which only makes me think they're saving up for some *total* bullshit later on."

Hanssen sighed. "Well, let's spread the word for everyone to stay on their guard—both against the corporates and the ANP. If we've been lucky with them so far, let's not slip up now."

Erlend grunted.

Chapter 25 - Price

"Hadamard was right," declared Admiral Ibuka.

The admirals were assembled in the situation room and examining the after action reports from Hadamard's intrusion into Hezokeen space. The results were indisputable, but they had still spent half an hour disputing them—if only to feel that the obvious conclusions had not been bought cheap.

Hadamard was right, Willoch repeated to herself, but he was also damned. He must have known when launching this operation that it would be professional suicide. If he had been wrong about the Hezokeen fleet movements, then his bold infiltration would have been a disaster and landed him in a court-martial. But, in the act of being proved right, he had conversely proved his superiors wrong, and that could only deal his career an equivalent death blow. Plus, all Hadamard had done was prove a fact that it did them little good to know: that the Hezokeen fleet was on the loose, perhaps four hundred ships strong, —perhaps on their doorstep—, and their only weapon was a little foreknowledge.

"The meaning of the second hypercomm signal at the start of the week is now clear," Ibuka continued. "It was a 'get set' code from the Hezokeen's planet-side agents. This prompted their fleet to evade our surveillance and move into a forward position. Now they must be waiting for a third signal, and that *will* be the final 'go' code."

"How far off do you suppose that is?" asked Lightman.

"Hard to say," offered Cao. "The Hezokeen spent several days scrambling after the second signal, which meant they expected a fair delay before receiving the third. ... So perhaps a week. That gives their fleet plenty of time to get into position, and yet the delay is not so long that they risk being discovered wherever they are."

"With five days passed since the second signal, that means we probably have only a few days more ... "

"But these are the *facts*," stressed Ibuka. "And, given them, our response is dictated. The fleets must go to their highest alerts at once. And, on the civilian side, evacuation plans must be made ready in every country."

"Speaking of mustering the fleets," asked Gould, "have we recalled Hadamard's group yet?"

"No," said Schleicher, Hadamard's commander. "But he reported that he could be back in thirty hours."

"Why so slow?"

"The *Jotunheim's* hyperdrive was damaged during the intrusion operation. Her top speed will be what's limiting them."

"Shall we have Hadamard escort the *Jotunheim* back, but only to the Monitoring Lines? Then, once they're inside of the grid, all of the healthy ships double-time it back to the fleet?" He glanced specifically at Willoch, who gestured her detached approval.

Despite the importance of this meeting, Willoch was vizsurfing through most of it and tending to her horrendous backlog of mail. She had already been swamped with work at the start of the week, and then the Lontan Governor's revelation about the Singularity AI had set off a firestorm across the Eyes governments. Suddenly they were all watching Norway like a fission bomb on a short fuse, and Willoch—as the highest-ranking Norwegian military officer—had become the nexus of their hysteria. She was being smothered with by-the-minute messages from admirals, generals, ministers, and THEACOMs ... She could almost feel the necklace of creeper subs and ballistic batteries deploying within range of Oslo, just in case the Eyes felt the need to squelch a Singularity Reprise.

She needed a break. Her mind was a cacophony of disaster plans, emergency contingencies, Hezokeen gambits, and worst-case scenarios. She quietly got up from her seat and left.

She walked, paying no attention to the course she picked. She set a fast pace to get her blood flowing. Heading in one direction, she quickly reached an exit of the military legation. When she stepped up to the door, however, it did not open automatically.

"Excuse me, ma'am?" asked a guard who was posted there. "Are— ... Are you sure you want to go out there?"

Willoch was too absorbed in thought to care what he said. She only waved at him and he released the door locks.

Stepping out, she found herself in a small passageway. It was well lit where she appeared, but in either direction the corridor was dotted with only sparse overhead lights, making it stutter into darkness. She turned left—the result of a mental coin flip—and ducked her head down. A rear-view OHUD window showed the guard stepping out of the door and looking after her.

A tense quiet hung in the corridors. Willoch did not think this foreboding, only that it well accommodated her contemplative state of mind. She walked quickly while seeing how soft she could make her footsteps.

Eventually she caught the scent of a mounting fetor on the air. A light was flickering up ahead, and closing in she saw a barrel nursing a fire. Several cloaked figures were gathered around it, propitiating their hands to the flames' warmth. This drew Willoch to finally notice the low temperature: it was briskly chilly. This section of the station was unheated.

Where was she? she finally thought to wonder. Granted she had never walked out of the military legation this way before, but she had never suspected that something seedy might await her.

Nearing the light, she realized that the people around the fire were one piece of a small village up ahead. Willoch wanted to turn away, but she thought that making an about-face this late would attract attention—and betray nervousness. She proceeded forward.

There were many bundled figures lying against the walls and sprawled on the floor. Most of the hallway doors were open, leaking out light and offering glimpses inwards. Willoch saw mothers cooking over makeshift open flames, children playing with broken toys, couples engaged in intimacies or altercations ... These disparate scenes were packed so tightly together, yet each seemed independent of the others. The homeless slept, the drifters warmed themselves, the domestics quarreled, and they all acted as if inside of their own universe. Even Willoch—a prim military officer strolling arrogantly through their ghetto—was left unmolested. The few who noticed her looked on remotely, as if there were an unbridgeable gulf between them.

Belatedly Willoch realized why she should not be walking in these levels. Ever since the depression, Gateway denizens had been steadily going bankrupt and finding themselves without even the money to buy a return ticket down the lev. Trapped in a tin can a hundred thousand kilometers in the air, they had collected in the station's unregulated basement, which happened to be around the military legation. Willoch had never seen these ghettos in person because she commuted on the direct express lifts. She accessed a map and plotted a course back towards the station's center—and civilization. It was a quick walk, and she encountered no more people.

She had just reached a lev lobby when she came upon a perplexing scene. There was a wide pool of rubbish in the middle of the floor, and a band of urchins was running around it. Each child was carrying a garbage bag, and with its contents they were strewing the ground like ecstatic petal-sowers. The eldest were ten years old, and they stood apart, issuing instructions to the younger ones. Puzzled and intrigued, Willoch stood back in the shadows, waiting for this madness to yield a method.

There was a whistle from one of the elders, then the little children scattered away from the garbage heap. Each found a hiding place near the intersection, but they remained giddy and giggling from the exercise. Vicious "Shhhh!"s came from all around until the troop was silenced. Willoch wondered what absurd game they were playing ...

Moments later a service lift pulled to a halt on their level. Its doors opened and a janitor wheeled out into the intersection. It paused to appraise the refuse heap, dissected it into an optimal collection route, and then proceeded to work. It started at an extreme end and began driving back and forth over the pile in lawnmower boustrophedon.

It was a third of the way through the heap when Willoch heard another whistle, and then the dozen children surged from their hiding places and rushed the janitor. The machine had no algorithms to recognize the *Lord of the Flies* scenario heading for it, so it only continued its paces.

The children screamed with delight as they jumped on top of the janitor, grabbing its garbage bag and pushing it over. The robot deployed grapples and feet to right itself, but the children restrained them. When the janitor finally realized that it was being hijacked, it let out a screeching tocsin, and a martial voice boomed from its speakers: "Warning! You are accosting Gateway Station property! Cease and desist as security is already responding to—"

The voice did not finish. Once the little children had upended the janitor, the older ones went to work on it with a torturer's array of screwdrivers, spanners, and auto-claws. Starting in at its ventral side, they pried off its covers, clipped its power lines, and were soon yanking out its innards as if goring a pumpkin. They worked feverishly but meticulously.

As the older children flung the janitor's bowels behind them, the younger ones collected the parts. Each was assigned some specific piece: one to collect the wheels, another a certain style of plastic hosing, another the circuit boards ... Once the janitor had been hollowed out, they ripped apart the chassis itself, and the children ran away clutching whole sections of its carapace.

In thirty seconds it was over. The only thing left of the janitor was its garbage bag.

Willoch marveled at it. The children had gutted the thing with the speed of a cheetah kill on the Serengeti, but also with the fastidiousness of Eskimos dismantling a whale husk. Every piece had been salvaged to some crucial use. And the children were probably now racing the parts back to their adult overseers, who would pay them scraps of food for these raw materials.

Five seconds later another lift pulled to a stop on the floor and a pair of station police came running out. They skidded to a halt before the garbage pile and the janitor's remains, and knew immediately that they were too late.

"Fuck, John!" shouted the first. "They are too fast at that shit ... "

"Oi!" the other yelled, looking around. "Get the fuck back here, you little runts!"

"John, they're *kids* ... " the first said.

"Fuckin' monsters is more like it."

"Yeah, they're already gone," said the first, apparently talking to HQ over comms—and forgetting to subvocalize. "... Shit, weren't *you guys* supposed to take all the janitors off this level? ... They're layin' traps for 'em down here, fer fuck's sake!"

"Lured 'em in with a janitor's wet dream," said John, kicking at the refuse.

223

The other guard saw Willoch. Surprised at seeing a uniform down in this sector, he yelled, "Hey! ... Whatcha doin' down here? ... Ma'am."

"Walking," said Willoch, simply.

Both men looked at each other. Under the circumstances, a totally unexpected response.

"Well, which way'd they go?" John asked.

"Take your pick, there were about a dozen of them."

"Shit ... " the police swore again, losing interest. They walked off down the corridor, and Willoch resumed her course.

A single hallway later she reached the wide-open plain of Gateway's central cylinder. This was the base of the spiral ramp that connected all thirty levels of the main trunk. Willoch stepped on and began the long trudge upwards. She lasted only four levels, however, before her age demanded rest. Then she stepped onto the up-conveyors that threaded the center of the ramp and it moved her along at a leisurely speed.

Willoch found her thoughts turning over that scene with the urchins. There was something there that she kept re-trafficking the details to find ... The tackling of the janitor, the apportioning of its parts, the glee on the children's faces ... Willoch had seen the signs of the depression everywhere: stagnation, retreat, collapse. But this struck her in a new way. Why was it distracting her so? ...

Soon she had it. Janitors were supposed to be elementary hardware, but now they were being hunted to feed a starvation economy. Humanity was eating its own tail.

And, for the first time in her life, Willoch started to wonder about the future of her people. And not just about whether the depression would end or not, but about what they could even do once it did.

She wanted Humanity to expand and grow, and she had always thought that they had the will to reach the stars. Was there not ample proof? They had gone to the heavens first all by themselves, and at such a terrific speed. From the Wright brothers to Neal Armstrong in only sixty-six years. That was a record of which few other civilizations could boast, even across the galaxies. 'We choose to go to the Moon,' the US President had said, 'not because it is easy, but because it is hard.' That was the essence of her species: they lived for meeting challenges and scaling heights. They toppled records one day, and on the next thought only of how they would topple them again. Granted they were still young and naive, but they were also ambitious, with such incredible feats within their reach. The Lontans had since accelerated their progress, but had not the essential spirit always been theirs?

And yet how could Humanity have such an indomitable will to explore if something as slight as the Singularity had sent them reeling. Even admitting how great a loss it had been for her personally—her capital city and her country—, how could it have set the world retreating on every front?

What was the destruction of Oslo to a New York stockbroker or a Shanghai tech magnate? They should have simply reshuffled their speculations and gone back to business. So why did it all stop?

The only reason she could see was the one it feared her to entertain: that perhaps Humanity had never really had the pioneer spirit she had thought. And there was ample proof here, as well. As impressive as the Moon landing had been, it had not been purely about exploration and advance. The President's speech might more honestly have said, 'We choose to go to the Moon, not because it is easy—nor even because we want to—but just to beat the Soviets there.' That summit achievement was really just a few countries engaged in typical one-upmanship. And there had been nothing special about going to the Moon, nor even the whole space race in general. It had only been a suitably prestigious way for the superpowers to match wits. Something more elaborate than chess, and of higher stakes than the Olympic Games.

Maybe that was how the Lontans had carried them to space: not because Humanity truly wanted to go there, but because each nation could not lose face before the others. The Lontans had sold them starships and space elevators by tickling their natural materialism and competitiveness. But Humanity had never chosen this future.

... And so that explained the Singularity. It had been the first time when they were forced to step back and honestly examine where they were headed. Suddenly realizing that this had never been their decision, they had stalled in limbo. And more than that they were rebelling against the alien way of life they had been tricked into adopting. They were sliding back into their aboriginal isolation.

So Humanity had failed the test of first contact. Because, even if they could magically end this depression, there was no guarantee that they would be able to deal with whatever came next. Of all the sentient species out there, only a fraction helmed the stars, so there had to be some qualifications for the post. Indeed, whatever had put the Lontans in their commanding position had to be more than just the accident of being born first. To still be here—and so many other places—a million years later must have taken a great will. To behold a manifest destiny as immeasurable and unconquerable as the universe itself and to think only, 'Now, where do we start ... '

Meanwhile, Human history painted at best a violent adolescence. Only a hundred years ago their species had committed its greatest atrocities, redefining the limits of inhumanity. And the century since had hardly been an act of contrition. Every age made its own vows about turning swords into plowshares—which then became the ironic recipe for framing their recidivism. Human wisdom grew only out of trial and error, their ingenuity was financed by perpetual distrust, and their survival was leased with mutually assured destruction. Granted this had served them thus far, but it was

clear that success on the infinite scale of the stars
would exact a much higher price.

Interlude - Figures

Janus was sweeping his arm back and forth, reciting the motion of an athlete preparing for a discus throw. But cradled in his hand—instead of a clay disc—rested a beer bottle, half full of water. Mohr was also standing at the roof's edge, and he had a zoomwindow open sighting the spot a block away that was Janus's target. It was a balcony five stories up in a residential building, distinguished by the teddy bear sitting on its railing. The bear's plush body was fetid and eaten away by years of exposure, making its glass eyes the only things left intact. The windows on a soul that prayed for death.

Janus stood some meters back from the ledge, allowing a run-up distance for his throw. He could not see his target directly from there, but his OHUD was rendering a simulated view that removed the obstructing buildings, giving him a clear line of sight.

High-rise beer bottle toss was one of the corporate army's favorite pastimes. The men were frequently granted liberty passes in Oslo, but then Oslo was unfortunately the only city in the world where there was nothing to do. Beer bottle toss was how the men had turned that emptiness into an asset.

"Aaaaany time," said Mohr, becoming impatient.

Janus ignored this botherance and continued gyring his arm back and forth. He was programming his muscles to hit their target, cinching his biological crosshairs ever tighter. The raw ballistics were already challenging enough, and then he also had to account for the wind. Visualizing the airflows in his OHUD, Janus was doing his best to divine a way through those shifting tides, but this was a job beyond even a top-of-the-line hypercomp. Of course, if the problem could be solved completely analytically, then it would not be interesting. Not Human.

By now Janus had achieved the proper readiness in his muscles. He had only to wait for the wind to present the right conduit for the toss. Patiently ... Patiently ... —There! His body sprang into its long-prepared action.

Mohr had two zoomwindows open in his OHUD: one fixed on the balcony, and another following the beer bottle in flight. It looked on track to find its target ... but started drifting slightly right ... and it shattered against the building facade only half a meter away from the balcony. A disappointment, but it was still the closest either of them had come to hitting a target that afternoon.

"Damn," commented Janus.

"A shame," added Mohr.

Before they could take another turn at bat, they had to empty another pair of beer bottles. They sat down, dangled their legs over the roof's edge, and cracked the last pair in the six-pack they had brought.

Mohr took time to breathe in the scene. The 'isolation drill' started tomorrow, and that would mean forty-eight hours cooped up inside of the Bunker. He needed this time out in the open air beforehand.

Surveying the street, he thought there was real beauty to the city's metamorphosis. Knots of verdure infested the sidewalks and grew out of every seam. The unkempt trees were reaching wildly high while their roots dulged up the concrete. And all the buildings were speckled with broken windows, as if they were smiling with blackened or missing teeth.

In his now well-developed tick, Mohr scratched at the back of his left hand, feeling for the patch of skin that held the nanoarray. And once again—as all the times before—it was textureless and smooth. No message from Kjaerstad.

Mohr was about to tell Janus. Nothing outright about what Kjaerstad had said or the nanoarray— that was impossible. He trusted Janus completely, but then Oslo was still hostile territory. It was planted thick with countless electronic eyes and ears that were piping everything back to the Bunker. There was probably even company spyware running in his own OHUD. Mohr could broach the subject with Janus only dimly, and even that would be a risk. But he needed a partner in crime, even if that

231

partner had not the vaguest idea what he was signing on for.

Mohr cleared his throat and said, "So ... I'm pretty sure something ... *strange* ... is going to happen."

Janus took a swig from his bottle and nodded. "I know what you mean."

Mohr glanced at him, surprised at his receptiveness. "You do?"

"It's pretty obvious. Everyone stacking up here in the Bunker. Garrisoning the place like the Russians are coming. This phony 'isolation drill.'" He huffed. "Something's headed for FUBAR."

That encouraged Mohr to skip to his denouement. He had thought long about how best to put this, but he was still stuck on his first draft. He said only:

"Well, if something strange does happen ... *we* may have to do something strange, too." That was it. That was all he could safely say.

And Janus replied, in bright matter-of-fact, "That figures." He finished off his beer and chucked the bottle outwards. They watched it arc down and smash on the street, spreading out into a thousand fragments of amber.

THE END